RICH AND HUMBLE

RICH AND HUMBLE

OLIVER OPTIC

WILDSIDE PRESS

INTRODUCTION

KARL WURF

William Taylor Adams (1822–1897), better known as "Oliver Optic," was one of the most widely read American writers of boys' stories in the nineteenth century. Born in Medway, Massachusetts, he taught in Boston public schools for about twenty years before writing full time. His classroom experience gave him a close view of boys' hopes and faults, and it shaped the brisk, moral adventures that made his name.

His breakthrough came with *The Boat Club; or, The Bunkers of Rippleton* (1855), which mixed boating adventure with lessons on honesty and teamwork. The book led to a full series and showed him the power of linked story cycles. Over the next decades he wrote more than a hundred volumes and a large body of short work for juvenile magazines and story papers.

Optic wrote in a world already rich in improving tales for the young, including the moral stories of Jacob Abbott and Samuel Goodrich. Like them, he stressed character, but he softened the sermon by using lively plots and familiar settings. A near-contemporary of Horatio Alger, Jr., he was later grouped with Alger, Harry Castlemon, and Martha Finley as an "Immortal Four" of juvenile series fiction.

Across school stories, nautical yarns, and Civil War adventures, his books praise industry, courage, and patriotism. Titles such as *The Soldier Boy; or, Tom Somers in the Army* place young heroes amid national events, while the "Young America Abroad" series uses travel to teach geography and manners.

Rich and Humble; or, The Mission of Bertha Grant was the first volume in the Woodville Stories, a six-book sequence "for boys and girls." Set in a comfortable river-town household, it contrasts worldly pride with practical charity and steady duty. Instead of wild melodrama, Optic relies on domestic scenes, small acts of kindness or cruelty, and the gradual testing of his young characters' principles.

Optic's popularity helped move American children's fiction away from stiff tracts toward more energetic, story-driven narratives. Ultimately, he paved the way for the more exciting books and series that followed, including *The Hardy Boys*, *Nancy Drew*, and many others.

Readers who enjoy this book's mix of everyday life and moral growth will find much to explore elsewhere in his work. *In School and Out; or, The Conquest of Richard Grant* follows a headstrong Woodville boy at school. *Poor and Proud; or, The Fortunes of Katy Redburn* shows a girl supporting an ailing mother, while *Now or Never; or, The Adventures of Bobby Bright* traces a boy's struggle to remain honest under pressure.

CHAPTER 1

A MISSIONARY TO THE HEATHEN

"Please give me ten dollars, father?" said Bertha Grant.

"Ten dollars!" exclaimed Mr. Grant, with a smile which looked very encouraging to the applicant. "What in the world do you want ten dollars for?"

"Oh, I want to use it, father."

"Well, I suppose you do. I have not the slightest doubt on that point."

"You are in a hurry now, father, and I will tell you all about it another time," replied Bertha, casting an anxious glance at her brother, who appeared to be an interested listener.

"Well, child, there is ten dollars," added Mr. Grant, as he handed her two half eagles.

"Now, dad, do only half as much as that for me, and I will be satisfied," said Richard Grant, the only brother of Bertha.

"Not a dollar, Richard. Where did you study politeness, my son? Dad! Do you think that is a proper term to apply to your father?"

"I meant papa," whined the boy, in affected tones of humility.

"If you ever call me 'dad' again, I will send you off to a boarding school to mend your manners. You ought to be ashamed of yourself."

"I am, papa, and I promise you I never will call you so again, though that is what all the fellows call their governors."

"Enough of this. I do not wish to hear any slang talk in my house. Don't call me 'dad,' or 'governor,' either; before my face or behind my back."

"I will not, papa."

"Nor papa, either. You need not be a little rowdy, nor a great calf."

"I will not, father. Now give me five dollars," whined the youth, as he extended his hand to receive the gift.

"Not a dollar, Richard!" replied Mr. Grant, sternly. "Money does you no good."

"I don't think that is fair, father," protested Richard. "When Bertha asks you for ten dollars, you give it to her. When I ask you for only five, you will not give it to me. If she had asked for twenty or fifty, you would have let her have it."

"Very likely I should," replied the father, so coolly that it was clear the argument of his son had not moved him.

"I think you are partial."

"You can think what you please, Richard."

"Why won't you give me money when I ask for it, as well as Bertha? I am older than she is, and I don't see why I should be treated like a baby."

"Because you act like one. When you behave like a man, you shall be treated like one."

"What have I done, father?"

"You have not done anything that is noble, generous or manly. You want five dollars to enable you to visit some bowling alley, billiard saloon or horse race."

"I don't want it for any such use."

"What do you want it for?"

"You did not ask Bertha what she wanted her money for; at least you did not make her tell you."

"I know very well she will apply it to a good use."

"Humph!" growled Richard. "She has gathered a crowd of beggars and paupers in the Glen, and she will waste the whole ten dollars upon them. I don't think it is very proper for her to associate with those dirty savages from the Hollow."

"It is more proper than to associate with the better-dressed savages from the other side of the river."

"Now won't you please let me have the five dollars, father?" pleaded Richard, who had a point to gain, and therefore was not disposed to carry his argument any further.

"I will not, Richard. I gave you five dollars the other day, and the next morning I heard that you had been seen with most disgraceful companions in a bowling saloon. Richard, if you have any respect for yourself, or regard for me and your sisters, do not associate with low and vile company."

As Mr. Grant uttered this earnest warning, he put on his hat and left the room. When he had gone, and the wayward son realized that his father fully understood his position, he threw himself upon the sofa with an exclamation of anger and resentment. It was evident that the warning he had received produced no effect upon him, and that he was only smarting under the pain of disappointment.

His father had so often given him money when he asked for it that he did not expect to be refused in the present instance, especially when he saw his sister so liberally supplied. He remained for a few moments upon the sofa, venting his anger and disappointment by kicking and crying, as a very small child does when deprived of some coveted plaything.

"That's too confounded bad!" exclaimed he, at last, rising from the sofa and walking toward Bertha, who had been a sad and silent spectator of the scene which had just transpired. "All my fun for the day is spoiled. Berty, won't you help me out of this scrape?"

"What scrape, Dick?"

"I want five dollars very badly. I must have it, too. I can't get along without it. I shall be a byword among all the fellows if I don't have it," added Richard, with a great deal of earnestness. "Lend me five dollars of the money father gave you, and I will pay you in a few days, when the governor is better natured."

"The governor?" suggested Bertha, with a reproving smile.

"Father, I mean, of course. What is the use of being so nice about little things. I never saw the old man in such a ferment before in my life."

"The old man?"

"There it is again!"

"I don't like to hear such names applied to father. It really hurts my feelings, and I hope you will not do so."

"Pooh! All the fellows call their fathers by these names. It sounds babyish to say 'my father'; and I don't like to be different from the rest of the fellows."

"I hope you will not be like the young men on the other side of the river with whom you associate."

"Nonsense! They are real good fellows. They don't go to the prayer meetings, it is true, but, for all that, they are better than hundreds that do go."

"I think they are bad boys, and I hope you won't go with them any more."

"Then it was you that told father I went with them," said Richard, suddenly stopping in his walk across the room, and looking his sister full in the face.

"I did tell him, Richard; but you know I did so for your good."

"Pooh! For my good! Do you think I cannot take care of myself?"

"I hope you can."

"I didn't think you were a little telltale, Berty," sneered Richard.

"I have spoken to you about going with those bad boys, and begged you to keep away from them. If you knew how bad I feel when I see my brother in such company, you would not complain of me for telling father."

"I won't complain, Berty," replied Richard, suddenly changing his tone. "You are a real good girl, and you intended to do me a heap of good when you told father. You are the best sister in the world. Now lend me the five dollars, Berty, and I never will find fault with you for anything you may do."

"I cannot, Richard."

"You cannot? Yes, you can. Haven't you got two half eagles in your hand?"

"I have, but I got them for a particular use."

"But I will pay you again."

"I suppose you will, if you can."

"If I can! Do you think dad—father, I mean—will always be as savage as he was this morning?"

"I am afraid you don't understand him, Richard. He thinks that giving you money does you injury."

"Don't preach any more, Berty. Will you lend me the five dollars?"

"I cannot. It would not be right for me to do so, even if I could spare the money."

"Why not?"

"Father refused to give it to you because he thought it would be an injury to you, and it would certainly be wrong for me to thwart his purpose."

"Then you won't let me have it?" demanded Richard, struggling to keep down his resentment.

"What are you going to do with it?"

"What odds does it make what I want it for?"

"If you want it for any good purpose I might let you have it," answered Bertha, who was wavering between a desire to oblige her brother and the fear of doing wrong.

"I want it to put in the contribution box for the Hottentots in the Sandwich Islands, of course," replied Richard, with a sneer.

"Tell me what you want it for Dick."

"Well, I scorn to lie about it. I offered to bet five dollars with Tom Mullen that our sailboat would beat his, and he has taken me up. The race is to come off today, and if I don't get the money I shall have to back down."

"I hope you will, Dick," said Bertha, sorrowfully. "What would father say if he knew you were betting on boats?"

"If he had any spunk at all he would hand out the money, and tell me to go it."

"You know very well he would disapprove of it. I think it is very wicked to gamble and bet."

"No preaching. Are you willing to have me tabooed as a sneak; to have me a byword and the laughingstock of the fellows?"

"I would rather have such fellows hate you than like you, Richard," answered Bertha, sadly. "I did not think you had gone so far as to gamble."

"Pshaw! There is no gambling about it. I am not going to be branded as a sneak. If you won't lend me the money, I must get it somewhere else."

"I cannot lend it to you, Richard, for such a purpose. You will be a disgrace to your family if you go on in this way."

"I should like to know what you are doing! Don't you spend half your time with those dirty savages from the Hollow? Do you think it is right for the daughter of Franklin Grant to associate with those dirty, filthy, half-civilized ragamuffins?"

"It will not injure either them or me."

"I am ashamed of you. If it does not hurt your feelings it does mine, to hear that you spend your time with these dregs of society. The fellows on the other side are all laughing at you."

"Let them laugh. While I do my duty, I need not fear them."

"Come, Berty, we won't quarrel. Let me have one of those half eagles, and I will let you go with the savages as much as you please."

"No, Richard," replied Bertha, shaking her head, with a smile which showed that there was no anger or resentment in her heart.

"Do, Berty!"

"I cannot; my conscience will not let me do so."

"Confound your conscience!" exclaimed Richard, rushing out of the room in a paroxysm of anger.

Bertha was sorely tried by the conduct of her brother. She had observed, with anxiety and pain, the dissolute course of Richard. She had reasoned and pleaded with him to abandon his wayward companions, but no good result had attended her efforts to reform him.

Mr. Grant was a broker in the city of New York. He had the reputation of being a very wealthy man. He lived upon a magnificent estate on the Hudson, about twenty-five miles from the city. His wife had been dead several years, and his three children were under the guidance of a housekeeper, who, though an excellent woman, did not possess a mother's influence, nor did she exercise a mother's authority over her young charge.

Woodville, the residence of the broker, was a beautiful place. The mansion and its appointments were all that wealth and taste could make them. Servants, without number, came and went at the bidding of the children. Tutors and governesses had been employed to superintend the education of the young people. Boats on the river, carriages on the land, were ever ready to minister to their inclinations. There was no end to the dogs, ponies, rabbits, monkeys, squirrels, deer and other pets which were supplied to beguile their leisure hours.

Mr. Grant believed himself to be a rich man, and none of his friends or neighbors had any reason to suspect he was not a rich man. He lived like a nabob; but more than this, he was a generous and kind-hearted man, and those who knew him best respected him most, while his wealth purchased for him the worldly esteem of all within the circle of his influence.

As my young readers have already discovered, he was an indulgent parent. Since the death of Mrs. Grant, his children had been his sole domestic happiness. He was wholly devoted to them; but his immense business transactions obliged him to be absent from an early hour in the morning till a late hour in the evening, and they were thus left, for the greater portion of the time, to the care of the housekeeper and their instructors.

Our story opens in the month of July, and it was vacation with the young people. The tutor and the governess had two months' leave of absence. Richard, Bertha and Fanny were free from the restraints of study. They had nothing to do but enjoy themselves. How Richard, who was fifteen years old, spent his time has already been shown.

Bertha, while wandering alone one May day in the Glen, a secluded valley on the bank of the river, half a mile from Woodville, had met a party of poor children from Dunk's Hollow, which is a little village a mile or more from the mansion house. There were seven of them, and they were children of the poorest people in the neighborhood. They were dirty, ragged, barefoot, and their condition excited the pity of the child of plenty.

She gave them the cake and confectionery she had brought to grace her lonely May-day festival in the Glen, told them stories, and made herself as agreeable as though she had been an angel sent to mitigate the woes of poverty and want. The event opened a new vista to Bertha, and she at once began to devise means to instruct these children of want and improve their worldly condition. Without going to a far-off land, she became a missionary to the heathen, the friend and companion of the needy and neglected. Despising the taunts of her brother and sister, she spent most of her leisure hours with her ragged disciples in the Glen.

CHAPTER 2

BERTHA FINDS HERSELF SHORT OF FUNDS

Woodville was situated on the right bank of the Hudson. About one mile above was the village of Dunk's Hollow, as it was called. It was only a small collection of houses, occupied by boatmen, fishermen and laborers—American, Irish and Dutch, all blended together in the most inharmonious manner.

Dunk's Hollow had a very bad name in the neighborhood, and man, woman or child who came from there was deemed a reproach to the race. There was only one shop at the Hollow, and that was the principal source of all its misery, for its chief trade was in liquor, pipes and tobacco. The oldest inhabitant could not remember the week in which there had not been at least one fight there, and the number was often half a dozen. The men did small jobs, and spent most of their earnings at the tap-room of Von Brunt, while the women maintained an almost ineffectual struggle to obtain food enough to keep themselves and their children alive. This was Dunk's Hollow, to whose poor and neglected little ones Bertha Grant had become a ministering angel.

On the opposite side of the river was the thriving village of Whitestone, in surprising contrast with the place just described. It contained four or five thousand inhabitants, with all the appointments of modern civilization, including a race course, half a dozen billiard saloons, where betting and liquor drinking were the principal recreations, and as many bowling alleys and fashionable oyster shops. All these traps to catch young men were frequented by the elite of the village, as well as by the sons of rich men, whose estates adorned the hills and valleys of the surrounding country. Here Richard Grant had taken his first lesson in dissipation.

About halfway between Woodville and the Hollow was the Glen. It was a beautifully shaded valley, on the bank of the river, through which a crystal brook from the hills above bubbled its way over the shining rocks to the great river. It was a fit abode for the fairy queens, and Bertha was a constant visitor at the spot, even before she made the acquaintance of the savages from Dunk's Hollow, as Richard persisted in calling them.

The Glen was situated in a curve of the river, which swept in from Woodville to the Hollow. Off the Cove, as it had been named, was a small island, containing not more than a quarter of an acre of land, called Van Alstine's. It was covered with rocks and trees, and was a frequent resort of boating parties, especially those from Woodville. This island, as well as the Glen, was owned by Mr. Grant, and he had taken some pains to clear up the underbrush and furnish it with seats and arbors.

Merry voices were heard in the Glen, even while the tones of anger and reproach were ringing in the lofty rooms of the mansion at Woodville. The savages from the Hollow were already gathered there, and the repeated glances which they cast down the river indicated the earnestness with which they expected the coming of their apostle of mercy. But Bertha was not ready to join them yet. The attitude of her brother was far from promising, and with a sad heart she realized that the heathen had invaded her own house.

After Richard rushed out of the house, angry and disappointed, her eyes filled with tears, and she tried to think of some method by which she could save him from the error of his ways. She knew that Tom Mullen and the other young men with whom her brother had lately begun to associate were the vilest of the vile. Tom had been seen intoxicated in the streets of the village, and it was well known that he and his companions were gamblers, if not thieves.

What could she do to save him? Alas! there was nothing that she, a child, could do; but she resolved never to cease pleading with him to reform. She wept and she prayed for him. She had faith to believe that He who lets not a sparrow fall unseen could save her brother from ruin and death, and with Him she pleaded that Richard might be redeemed.

Bertha's heart was full of love and gentleness; and while she wept over her brother, she rejoiced in the little flock to whom she had been the messenger of so many blessings. She had taught them to read, and imparted to them that wisdom which is higher and purer than any which flows from earthly fountains. As she thought of them, she glanced at the two gold pieces in her hand, and a smile lighted up her sweet face, when she imagined the pleasure they would purchase for the lambs of her fold.

Taking her hat and shawl, she left the house and walked down to the boathouse. It was located on the bank of the river, by the side of a small wharf extending out into the deep water.

"Waiting for you, Miss Bertha," said the old boatman, who had been told to row her over the river.

"I am all ready, Ben," replied Bertha, as she took her seat in the boat.

"What ails Mr. Richard this morning?" continued Ben, as he glanced at the sailboat, which was moored in the river a short distance from the shore, and in which Richard was seated, looking very gloomy and dejected. "He is uncommon cross this morning."

"Something happened at the house which did not please him."

"I thought so. He wanted to borrow five dollars of me; but I could not lend it to him, for I did not happen to have it about me. I am sorry Mr. Richard feels so bad."

"I hope he will feel better," replied Bertha.

"He tried to borrow the money of the cook, and of the hostler, but none of them had so much about them. Wouldn't his father let him have the money?"

"He would not. But I am all ready, Ben," said Bertha, who was very willing to change the subject.

"Where are you going, Bertha?" called Richard from the boat.

"Over to Whitestone."

"Wait a moment, and I will go with you," replied Richard, as he pulled ashore in his skiff. "What are you going to do over at Whitestone?" he asked, as he stepped into the boat.

"I am going over to buy some things."

"For the savages, I suppose," sneered Richard.

"Yes," answered Bertha, unmoved by the sneer. "If you knew how much pleasure my work affords me, you would want to join me."

"I think not; I would not disgrace my family by mixing with the slime and filth of the Hollow. Your ragged disciples stole half the strawberries in the garden last night."

"Not my children, I know."

"I will bet five dollars they were the same ones to whom you taught the Ten Commandments and 'Now I lay me,'" laughed Richard.

"I am sure it was none of mine. We are ready, Ben. You can push off. I feel like rowing a little this morning, and I will take one oar, if you please."

Bertha placed her reticule and shawl on the seat in the stern, and seated herself at one of the oars. Ben pulled a gentle stroke to accommodate that of Bertha, and the boat moved forward toward Whitestone. Richard kept bantering his sister all the way about the savages of the Hollow, and seemed to have entirely recovered from his disappointment and anger. In about half an hour they reached Whitestone. Bertha put on her shawl, and, taking her reticule in her hand, walked up to the principal street of the village, while Richard departed in another direction.

Bertha stopped at a dry goods store, where she bought two pieces of cheap calico, some jean and a number of other articles, amounting to ten dollars and fifty cents.

"Dear me!" exclaimed she, as she put her hand into her reticule; "I have lost all my money!"

"Lost your money?" said the salesman.

"I had two half eagles in my reticule, and both of them are gone," added she, looking upon the floor and searching the bag again. "I have not opened the reticule since I started from home, and I am sure they could not have fallen out."

"Didn't you put them in your pocket?"

"No; I am sure I put them in my bag. But it cannot be helped. Of course I cannot take these things now."

"Oh, yes, you can. You are Mr. Grant's daughter, and I shall be glad to give you credit for any amount you may desire."

"Thank you, sir. Then I will take the things and pay you for them the next time I come to Whitestone."

"Any time, Miss Grant. I will send them down to your boat."

But Ben had followed her up from the wharf, and carried the goods down for her. On their way to the river she told him that she had lost her money.

"Did you lose it in the boat?"

"I don't know where I lost it. I am sure I put it into my bag, which has not been opened since I left the house."

"I saw you put the reticule on the seat in the stern. Mr. Richard sat there all the way coming over."

Bertha blushed at these words, and looked earnestly at the boatman to discover what he meant by them; but Ben looked perfectly blank.

"Perhaps I dropped them out before I fastened the reticule," added Bertha.

"Perhaps you did, Miss Bertha; but—"

Ben stopped after the "but," and looked upon the ground, as though he had made a mistake. Bertha's face was crimsoned with shame, as she thought what that terrible "but" might mean. Richard had sat upon the bag containing the money during the passage across the river. Ben had taken pains to state this fact in so many words. What could he mean by it?

When they reached the wharf they found Richard in the boat, ready to return with them.

"Come, Berty; I have been waiting this half hour for you," said he; "I am in a hurry."

"Going to have the race today, Mr. Richard?" asked Ben, as he placed the bundle of goods in the bow of the boat.

"Yes, certainly. I told you yesterday it would come off today at eleven o'clock," answered Richard.

"You told me there was some little difficulty about the matter this morning," added Ben, with a smile, which was intended to remove any appearance of impudence which the words might otherwise convey.

"I have got over that difficulty, and am all ready for the race. We shall have a good wind today, and I am just as certain that I shall win the race as I am that I sit here. Bear a hand, Ben; I am in a hurry."

"Then you raised the money, Mr. Richard?" said Ben, carelessly, as he adjusted his oars.

"To be sure I did. I told you there were a dozen persons who would be glad to lend it to me. Bob Bleeker lent me ten dollars, though I did not ask him for but five."

"There!" exclaimed Ben, suddenly rising up and slapping his hands upon his trousers pockets; "I have forgotten my tobacco, and I shall die a thousand deaths without it. Will you excuse me for five minutes, Miss Bertha?"

"Certainly, Ben."

"Hurry up," added Richard.

"I will be back in less than five minutes;" and Ben ran up the wharf as if the house of his dearest friend had been on fire.

He rushed up one street and then turned into another, which brought him to the Empire Saloon, of which Mr. Bob Bleeker was the owner and proprietor. Taking a two-dollar bill from his wallet, he bolted into the saloon and thrust it into the face of the keeper of the establishment.

"What is the matter, Ben? You are all out of wind," said Bob, as he glanced at the two-dollar bill.

"Mr. Richard wants you to give him a better bill for this one," replied Ben, puffing like a porpoise from the effects of his hard run.

"A better bill? What does he mean by that?"

"You know all about it. Didn't you just give him this bill?"

"No, sir! I did not," replied Bob, quick to resent any trick, or any imputation of unfairness. "I did not give him that bill, or any other."

"Did you lend him ten dollars just now?"

"No, sir! I did not!" answered Bob, with emphasis.

"Then I have made a bad blunder, and I beg your pardon."

"All right, Ben."

"Give me half a pound of that best Cavendish, and I will call it square."

Ben having obtained his tobacco, which he had really forgotten, hastened back to the boat. Taking his place at the oars, he pulled his steady, even stroke, which in a short time brought them within hail of the Woodville wharf, where the boatman, without any apparent reason, suddenly suspended his labor, and the boat soon came to a dead halt.

"What are you stopping for, Ben?" demanded Richard. "You may put me on board of the *Greyhound*, if you please."

"Not yet, Mr. Richard. When I get into a fog, I always stand by, and wait till I can see my way out of it."

"What do you mean by that, Ben?"

"Hold on a minute, Mr. Richard, and I will make the daylight shine through what I have said in a very short time."

"Bear a hand, then, Ben, for you know I am in a hurry."

"So am I," added Bertha.

"Miss Bertha lost ten dollars in this boat, which goes right against my conscience."

"Perhaps I lost it in the house," suggested Bertha.

"Perhaps you did, but—" And Ben made a long pause before he added: "I don't believe you did."

"Well, what has all this to do with me, Ben?" asked Richard, his face as red as Bertha's had been.

"Not much, perhaps, but I don't want Miss Bertha to think now, or at any future time, that I took the money."

"Of course I don't think any such thing, Ben," added Bertha, reproach-fully.

"But you may think so at some future time, if the matter isn't cleared up now."

"I certainly shall not, Ben," interposed Bertha. "Please don't keep me here, when all my children are waiting for me in the Glen."

"Only a minute, Miss Bertha. I did not take your money; but—"

"Another 'but,' Ben," said Richard. "If you have got anything to say, why don't you say it?"

"I will say it," replied Ben, as he proceeded, in the most mysterious man-ner, to turn all his pockets inside out, to open his wallet, and shake out his handkerchief. "The half eagles are not in my pockets, you see."

"Ben, you are a fool!" exclaimed Richard.

The boatman seated himself again, and gazed in silence upon the bottom of the boat.

CHAPTER 3

BERTHA MAKES A VISIT TO THE GLEN

"You don't understand me, Mr. Richard," said Ben, after he had mused for a time.

"I'm sure I do not. You act as though you had lost your senses," replied Richard.

"But I have not lost my conscience, Mr. Richard. Perhaps you would not object to exhibiting the contents of your pockets."

"Do you mean to insult me, Ben?" exclaimed Richard, reddening with indignation.

"No, sir, certainly not; but you will do me a great favor by turning your pockets out—just to oblige an old servant of the family."

"Enough of this, Ben. Use your oars again."

"Excuse me, Mr. Richard, but I am in earnest. That money was lost in this boat. I am a poor man, and it must be found before any suspicion rests upon me."

"Ben, do you mean to say I took the money from my sister?"

"That is precisely what I mean, Mr. Richard, only I couldn't say it out in so many words, because you are the only son of Mr. Franklin Grant, the rich broker of New York. I thank you for helping me out with the idea."

"Oh, no, Ben! You must be mistaken. Richard would not do so mean a thing."

"I beg your pardon, Miss Bertha, but your brother did do this mean thing and if he is mean enough to steal ten dollars, which was to be given in charity, he is mean enough to lay it to the old boatman; and I will not risk myself on shore till the matter is cleared up."

"Ben, do you know who and what you are?" said Richard, sternly.

"I know all about it, Mr. Richard. I am your father's servant—your servant, if you please; but if I lose my place, and am sent to jail for what I do, I will have this matter set right before I go ashore."

"It is all right now, Ben. Put me on board of the *Greyhound*, and I will say nothing more about it."

"I will not. You stole the money from your sister, and you shall return it to her before you get out of this boat."

"Let him go, Ben," remonstrated Bertha, who began to be alarmed by the stern manner of the old boatman.

"I would do anything in the world for you, Miss Bertha, but I must have justice done in this matter."

"Nonsense, Ben. I haven't got the money," said Richard, who was also a little alarmed at the determined manner of the boatman.

"You have got it, Mr. Richard, and you must give it up."

"I say I have not got it. Doesn't that satisfy you?"

"It does not. If you haven't got it, you will not object to turning out your pockets."

"I have got ten dollars, of course. I told you I had."

"Where did you get it?"

"Didn't I tell you that I borrowed it of Bob Bleeker?"

"You didn't borrow a dollar of Bob Bleeker," answered Ben, placing himself by the side of the youth.

"Dare you tell me that I lie?"

"I dare tell you anything that is true. Will you show me the contents of your pockets or not?"

"I will not," replied Richard, stoutly.

The boatman made no reply, but, taking Richard by the collar, he jerked him into the middle of the boat, and, in spite of his kicks and struggles, thrust his hand into the boy's coat pocket, and took therefrom his portemonnaie. He then released him, and opened the wallet.

It contained two half eagles!

"Here is the money you lost, Miss Bertha."

"Why, Richard Grant!" exclaimed Bertha, "how could you do such a thing?"

"That is not your money, Berty. I borrowed it of Bob Bleeker," stammered Richard, whose face was now as pale as a sheet.

"Mr. Richard, would you be willing to go over with me and ask Bob Bleeker if he lent you ten dollars?"

"Of course I would if I had the time."

"Sit down, Mr. Richard, and I will tell you a story," and Ben proceeded to relate what had occurred in the saloon of Bob Bleeker. "Are you satisfied, Miss Bertha?"

"I am. Oh, Richard, how could you do such a thing!"

"I didn't do it."

"Let me see the half eagles, Ben. I remember the date of one of them, and I looked at them so much that I think I should know them again."

Ben handed her the gold pieces, and she was forced to acknowledge that they were the coins she had lost. The one whose date she remembered had a spot upon it, which enabled her to identify it.

"Oh, Richard!" said she, bursting into tears. "I did not think you had sunk so low! What will become of you?"

"I suppose I must run away and go to sea, or do something of that kind. My reputation is spoiled here."

"Oh, no, Richard! Promise to be a better boy, and Ben and I will not say a word about this."

"Ben has insulted and outraged me."

"Sorry for it, Mr. Richard, but I couldn't help it. The matter is cleared up now, and I haven't anything more to say."

"You will not mention this, Ben—will you?" pleaded Bertha. "Dick is sorry for it, and he will always be a good boy."

"I never talk about family matters, Miss Bertha. Whatever happens, I shall never say a word about this affair," replied Ben, as, with a few vigorous strokes of his oars, he placed the boat alongside the *Greyhound*.

Richard, stupefied at the suddenness with which his guilt had found him out, stepped mechanically from one boat into the other, hardly knowing what he was doing. Not only had he been convicted of the base act of stealing from his sister, but he was deprived of the means of attending the race. He felt as if some terrible disaster was impending, and threw himself into the stern sheets of his boat and covered his face with his hands.

"Now, Miss Bertha, I will row you up to the Glen in double-quick time."

"I don't like to leave Richard now. He must feel dreadfully."

"I hope he does. It will do him good to spend a few hours upon the stool of repentance. Leave him to himself for a while, Miss Bertha."

"But perhaps he will do some desperate thing, Ben. He may run away, as he threatened."

"No he won't. He hasn't the courage to run away. He knows what going to sea means, and a young gentleman like him won't do any such thing," said Ben, as he bent upon his oars, and the boat glided away in the direction of the Glen.

In a few moments Ben landed his fair young charge in the midst of her anxious disciples.

"Now, if you like, Miss Bertha, I will pull back and keep an eye on Mr. Richard."

"Do, Ben."

"Shall he stay about home today?" asked Ben, with a quiet smile on his bronzed features.

"You cannot keep him at home if he chooses to go away."

"Oh, yes, I can, Miss Bertha," answered the boatman, confidently. "If you only say the word, Miss Bertha, he shall stay at home and he will mind me just like a whipped kitten."

"Don't be too hard with him, Ben."

"Oh, bless you, no! I will handle him as gently as I would a basket of eggs; but he shall mind me, if you say the word. It is none of my business, but I don't like to see a fine boy, like Master Richard, going to ruin and destruction for the want of a steady hand at the helm."

"Do as you think best, Ben, but don't let any harm come to him."

"I won't, Miss Bertha," replied the boatman, as he shoved off and pulled toward Woodville.

Ben had once been a boatswain in the navy, and was accustomed to rigid discipline. He understood Richard's case exactly, and he had often regretted that he was not authorized to train him up in the way he should go. The father was ignorant of his dissolute life, and the boatman entertained some doubts whether Mr. Grant had the nerve to discipline him as the case demanded. Bertha was a power and an influence at Woodville, and Ben knew that whatever she counseled would be ratified at headquarters.

Richard was still lying on the cushions of the *Greyhound* when Ben returned from the Glen. Without seeming to notice the young reprobate, the boatman kept one eye upon him, while his hands were busied in carving a snake's head upon the end of a new tiller for the four-oar boat. There we will leave them, the watcher and the watched, and return to the Glen.

"We thought you never would come," said one of the little savages, as Bertha walked up to the Retreat with them.

The Retreat was an arbor, which was completely covered with vines, and in which seats had been built by the ingenuity of Ben, the boatman, who was almost as much interested in Bertha's mission as she was herself.

"Now, take your seats, children. I hope you have all got your lessons well, for we have a great deal to do today."

In a moment each of the little savages took a seat, and produced the book which Bertha had furnished. They read, spelled and recited arithmetic to the entire satisfaction of the teacher. New lessons were assigned for the next day, and then Bertha proceeded to open the bundles of dry goods.

"Here is a calico dress for each of the girls, and here is some jean to make jackets and trousers for the boys. We must be as busy as bees, and have them all made up this week."

The eyes of the little boys and girls sparkled with delight at this display of treasures. A Broadway belle or a Chestnut Street dandy could not have been more enraptured at the latest importation from Paris, than the poor children of Dunk's Hollow were at the sight of the homely material of which their new clothes were to be made.

But the most serious part of the work was yet to be done, and consisted in the cutting and fitting of the garments. Ever since the brilliant idea of supplying her flock with new clothes had entered the fertile brain of Bertha, she had studied and practiced the dressmaker's art, under the tuition of Mrs. Green, the housekeeper, who had kindly afforded her all the instruction she needed. She had also procured patterns for the jackets and trousers, and patiently examined some of her brother's old clothes, for she was determined that the outfit of the savages should be fashioned entirely by her own hands.

With a confidence worthy the pioneer mind of a Columbus, she tore off the breadths for the dresses, and set the girls at work in running them together. Then, with the same zeal and self-possession, she proceeded to fit the waist of Gretchy von Brunt, who was about as thick as she was long, and not exactly a model of female elegance in form. It was a trying experiment for a beginner, but for what the chief operator lacked in skill and experience, she made up in zeal and hope.

At twelve o'clock Ben came up with a basket of provisions for the busy troop of workers. He reported that Richard was as tame as a lamb, and had gone in to dinner when the bell rang. He did not think there was any danger of his doing a desperate deed. But Bertha insisted that he should return, and not lose sight of him till his father came home from the city. As he had been instructed in the morning, Ben brought up Bertha's boat, in which she intended to row back herself, when the labors of the day were finished.

While the girls were busily engaged upon their dresses, and the boys were bringing stones to make a walk from the landing place to the Retreat, a slight rustling was heard in the bushes, near the spot where the dinner things had been left.

"Hoo! Hoo! Hoo!" were the cries which immediately issued from the bushes.

It sounded like the scream of some wild bird; but neither Bertha nor her flock were frightened by the noise, though all of them left their work, and hastened to the spot from which it proceeded.

"It's Noddy Newman," said Griffy von Grunt, the largest of the three boys composing the mission school—a stout, fat little Dutchman of ten years of age.

"He has stolen what was left of the dinner," added Bridget McGee.

"And he will steal Miss Bertha's boat," said Billy Ball, as he and Griffy hastened down to the landing place, intending by a flank movement to protect the property of the mistress.

"He may have the dinner, if he will not carry off the basket and the plates," added Bertha. "Noddy! Noddy! Come here a moment; I want to see you," called she, as loud as she could.

"No, you don't," replied the wild boy who had caused this sudden commotion. "None of your spelling books for me. I like your dinner, but I don't want any of your learning."

Noddy Newman was now in view of the party. He was even more ragged and dirty than the raggedest and dirtiest of the Dunk's Hollowites. He wore nothing but a shirt and trousers with one suspender, and a straw hat, of which less than one-fourth of the original brim remained. Though he was said to be thirteen years old, he was smaller in stature than Griffy von Grunt; but he was as agile and quick as a monkey.

Noddy had no parents. They had lived at the Hollow till filth and dissipation ended their days. Since their death Noddy had taken care of himself; sleeping in barns and outbuildings at night, and begging or stealing food enough to keep him alive.

"Come to me, Noddy," repeated Bertha. "I won't hurt you."

"I know you won't. You can't!" shouted the wild boy, as he bounded off, with the speed of an antelope, toward the river, ending his flight by running up a large tree which overhung the water.

CHAPTER 4

BERTHA AND NODDY NEWMAN

Beneath the tree in which Noddy Newman had taken refuge lay moored a nondescript craft, in which the wild boy made his aquatic excursions. It had once been a sugar box, and by what art or skill the little savage had made it watertight it would have puzzled the calkers and gravers of the region to determine. It certainly floated, and Noddy navigated it about the river with as much pride and satisfaction as if it had been the fairy barge of Cleopatra. It was fastened by a string to one of the overhanging branches of the tree in which its adventurous skipper was now lodged.

It was pretty evident, from the position of his boat, that he had not landed in the ordinary way, but had drawn himself up into the tree and come ashore in that manner. To Bertha and her young companions it was a daring undertaking to embark in the sugar box by the way of the tree, and she begged him not to attempt it.

"Come down, Noddy, and I will put you into your boat."

"I ain't one of your children. I don't have anything to do with your reading and spelling, and you needn't borrow any trouble about me."

"But some of the branches are rotten, and if you should fall upon the rocks below, it would kill you."

"I ain't going to fall. I know better than that without any book l'arnin'."

"Do come down, Noddy. I will give you something if you will," pleaded Bertha, who, besides being alarmed for his safety, wished to converse with him, and induce him to join the school in the Glen.

Noddy had thus far resisted all overtures in this direction, and had never allowed himself to come near enough to Bertha to enable her to exercise any influence upon him. He was fond of his freedom, and evidently enjoyed the vagabond life he led. The authorities of Whitestone had once made an effort to commit him to the almshouse; but when an attempt was made to catch him, he disappeared for some weeks.

Bertha had sent him several presents, with messages urging him to join her little flock; but he never came to the Glen when she was there, unless it was to rob the basket of the provisions brought for the scholars. Yet she did not abandon all hope of winning him over from the savage life he led.

"Have you had dinner enough, Noddy?"

"Yes, I have. I ate all there was in the basket," replied Noddy, chuckling with delight at the thought of his own cleverness.

"Won't you come down and talk with me? I will give you something."

"I don't want anything."

"Come down and talk with me, then."

"I haven't got anything to say," laughed Noddy.

"But I want to see you."

"I don't want to see you. You are the proud girl from Woodville, and I don't want anything of you."

"I am not proud, Noddy."

"Well, you are rich."

"Come down to me, and I will give you a silver ten-cent piece."

"Don't want it; if I should go to buy anything with it they would catch me and put me in the workhouse."

"Don't you want a knife? I will give you mine, if you will go up to the arbor with me."

"I have got a better knife now than you have. I took it from Bob Bleeker's boat."

"But it was wrong to take it without leave."

"I don't know but it was. If it was I can't help it."

As he spoke these words, Noddy began to move down to the branch from which he could drop into his boat. As he did so, a rotten limb, which he had grasped with his hands, suddenly snapped, his feet slipped from the branch, and he fell, striking with such force upon the sugar-box craft that one of its sides was split off. The unfortunate boy rolled from the boat, and went into the deep water. A sharp cry issued from his mouth as he struck the board, and then he disappeared beneath the surface of the river.

"Mercy!" screamed Bertha, paralyzed with horror, as she witnessed the sad mishap.

"Never fear, Miss Bertha; he can swim like a fish," said Griffy von Grunt.

"But the fall may have killed him," gasped Bertha, as she summoned strength enough to run to her boat, which was moored a short distance from the spot.

At the same time, Griffy leaped into the river, and swam to the sugar box. In a moment Noddy rose to the surface; but he did not attempt to swim, and it was evident that the fall had deprived him of the use of his powers. As he rose, Griffy seized him by the arm, and held him above the water till Bertha came up with the boat. With no difficulty they lifted him in; but the little savage appeared to be dead. On his temple there was a deep cut, which had probably been caused by the nails driven into the side of the box to answer for thole pins.

"What shall we do?" stammered Bertha, terribly frightened by the pale face and motionless form of the poor boy. "I will take him down to the house. Griffy, you may go with me, and the rest of you may go home."

The children were appalled by the fearful accident, and could not say a word. Only Griffy seemed to have his wits about him, and while Bertha attempted to bind up the bleeding head of Noddy, he rowed with all his might toward the pier at Woodville. Ben was in the boathouse when they arrived, and, taking the insensible boy in his arms, carried him up to the house and laid him upon the bed in Bertha's chamber.

"Now, Ben, go over to Whitestone as fast as you can and bring the doctor."

"Yes, Miss Bertha; but I don't think the boy is very badly hurt. That knock on the head has taken away his senses; but he will be all right in a few hours. You can't kill a boy like that so easily."

"Go quick, Ben. I am afraid he is dead now."

"Oh, bless you! no, he isn't. Don't be frightened, Miss Bertha. Here comes Mrs. Green."

The housekeeper's opinion coincided with that of the boatman, that Noddy was not dangerously injured. She was an experienced nurse, and proceeded to take such measures for the relief of the sufferer as the case required. Before the doctor arrived the patient began to exhibit some signs of consciousness. He opened his eyes, and gazed around the room with a bewildered stare. The costly furniture was in strong contrast with anything he had ever before seen, and it was no wonder that he was bewildered.

As if conscious that he was not in his proper element, he suddenly attempted to rise, but sank back upon the bed with a deep groan, and closed his eyes again. The arrival of the doctor was gladly welcomed by Bertha. After a patient examination, he declared that the boy was badly hurt; that three of his ribs were fractured, and that he was probably injured internally.

Before evening Noddy was in full possession of his senses, but was suffering intense pain. Bertha remained by his side, ministering to all his wants with as much zeal and interest as though the patient had been her own brother.

When Mr. Grant came home, he found his daughter bending over the sick bed of the friendless outcast; and then, more than ever before, he realized what a treasure he possessed in this darling child. Richard was proud and haughty, but Bertha was a friend to the poor; humble even in possession of all the luxury and splendor which the world can afford.

Mr. Grant listened with pleasure to Bertha's narrative of the events of the day. Of the conduct of her brother in the morning she said nothing, for she had decided to wait till necessity compelled her to do so. She hoped Richard would reform his life, and, as he had given up the race, she was encouraged to believe that he was taking the first steps toward amendment.

The next day Noddy was feverish, and for a week he suffered a great deal. Bertha took care of him most of the time during the day, while Ben and the housekeeper attended him at night. Every day the boatman brought the children of the school from the Glen to the house, where, with the assistance of Mrs. Green and the chambermaids, the garments of the boys and girls were completed, and as soon as Noddy began to improve, Bertha gave them a picnic on Van Alstine's Island.

But the sick boy was not willing that his little nurse should leave him. His severe sickness seemed to have produced a wonderful effect upon him. It softened his heart, and made him more human than he had ever been before. He had become strongly attached to Bertha, and listened attentively to the gentle lessons of wisdom with which she improved the hours of his convalescence.

It was a fortnight before he was able to sit up, and a month before he could go out of the house; but much of the spirit of his life and character had returned to him, and he longed for the health and strength which would enable him to roam the fields and forests, and sail upon the river, as he had done before his fall.

"I shall be so glad to be well again!" exclaimed he, as he walked on the lawn one day with Bertha.

"What will you do then?"

"I shall run and climb and sail as I used to do; but I will go to your school, Miss Bertha."

"Don't you want to do something better than spend your time in idleness?"

"What can I do?"

"You can learn to be a useful and respectable man."

"I don't think I shall ever be of any use to anyone but myself. It was queer that I fell that day, after I had told you I knew enough not to fall."

"It was all for the best, Noddy."

"I don't believe that. How could it be best for me to stave in my ribs, and lie here, like a fool, for a month?"

"Perhaps it will prove to be the best thing that ever happened to you."

"You don't mean so, Miss Bertha," said the pale boy, with a smile.

"I do, Noddy. Our misfortunes are blessings to us; and we ought to be as thankful for them as for the prosperity we enjoy. If you had continued your wild life much longer, you would probably have been taken up and sent to prison."

Noddy made no reply, but kept thinking of what Bertha had said. He could not fully comprehend such wisdom, though he could not help believing that his coming to Woodville was a great event in his life. His fair instructress improved the advantage she had obtained, and the little savage was already more than half civilized.

During the month that Noddy had been confined to the house, Richard did not once visit Whitestone, or meet any of his former dissolute companions; but whether this was from mortification at his failure to sail the *Greyhound* with Tom Mullen, or because he had really commenced upon a new life, was a matter of painful doubt to Bertha. His father steadily refused to supply him with money, and he spent most of the time at home. He would not permit any allusion to the half eagles, either by his sister or the boatman.

He was gloomy and taciturn. When he used the *Greyhound*, he did not go near the other side of the river, and carefully avoided meeting any other boats, especially those belonging to Whitestone. One day, as he was sailing near the island, he observed a great commotion on board of a passing steamer, and soon ascertained that a man had fallen overboard. Trimming his sails, he bore down upon the spot, and succeeded in saving the stranger from a watery grave.

In the gratitude of his heart, the gentleman presented him with fifty dollars in gold, as he landed him on the pier at Whitestone, where the steamer had made a landing.

"Your name, young man," said the gentleman.

"John Green," replied Richard, after some hesitation.

"God bless you, John Green! I shall remember your name as long as I live," added the stranger, as he shook him warmly by the hand, and hastened on board of the steamer.

"John Green!" muttered Richard to himself, as he turned the bow of his boat toward Woodville, "I'm rich now, and that boat race shall come off yet."

If anyone had asked Richard why he had given a false name to the gentleman whose life he had saved, his pride would not have permitted him to acknowledge the meanness of the motive which prompted the falsehood. It was that he might conceal the fact of possessing so large a sum of money from the family at Woodville.

The next day, the *Greyhound* made another visit to Whitestone, and the terms of the contest between the two boats were arranged. Richard excused his long absence upon the plea that he had been sick, and his graceless companions were too glad to see him again to find much fault. The race was to take place in three days, and the stakes were placed in the hands of Bob Bleeker, who was to act as umpire upon the great occasion.

On the day before the race, Richard had the bottom of the *Greyhound* cleaned, her sails and ropes carefully adjusted, and everything done that would add a particle to his chance of winning the regatta. This time he kept his own counsel, and did not even tell Ben of the coming race.

The fifty dollars in his pocket had wrought a great change in the manner of Richard. He was no longer dull and gloomy, but full of life and energy. None of the family or the servants knew it was he who had saved the stranger from drowning, and, with all the neighborhood, had wondered who John Green was. No one had ever heard of him before, and the more they wondered, the more Richard chuckled over his own cunning and deception.

When Richard had completed his preparations for the race, he sat in the stern sheets of the *Greyhound*, thinking of the triumph he was so confident of winning.

"Richard! Richard!" called Bertha from the pier.

"What do you want, Berty?"

"Father hasn't come home."

"Well, what of it?"

"The train has arrived, and he did not come in it. Where do you suppose he is?" continued Bertha, as she stepped into her boat, and rowed to the *Greyhound*.

"I don't know. Perhaps he was talking politics, and forgot to get out at the station," replied Richard, indifferently.

"No; Mr. Barton said he was not in the cars."

"He is safe enough."

"He has looked very sad and troubled for several days. I am afraid something has happened," added Bertha, as she pulled back to the wharf.

CHAPTER 5

GOOD NEWS AND BAD

The return of her father from the city was a happy event to Bertha, and she was always the first to greet him on his arrival. It was an everyday occurrence, but it lost none of its interest on this account. He was the only parent she had, and his smile, as she welcomed him home, was worth all the watching and waiting which it cost.

When, therefore, on that eventful evening, the man who had gone to drive him up from the railroad station returned without him, gloomy forebodings filled her mind. Her father was very regular and methodical in his habits, and had never missed a train, or remained away overnight without announcing his intention to do so beforehand. This fact, added to the sad and anxious look which Mr. Grant had worn for several days, was enough to awaken painful thoughts, even in a mind less sensitive than that of Bertha.

The long, gloomy night wore away without any tidings from the absent father. Richard slept, and Fanny slept, but Bertha scarcely closed her eyes, so deeply was she impressed with the dread of some coming calamity. Long before sunrise, she left her chamber, and wandered up and down the walks upon the lawn, trying to make herself believe that nothing had happened to her father.

"Why, Miss Bertha, how pale you are this morning!" exclaimed Noddy, as he met her on the lawn, after the first bell had rung. "Are you sick?"

"No, Noddy, I am not sick."

"What ails you, then? Is it because your father did not come home last night?"

"Not because he did not come home, but because I fear something has happened to him."

"Well, I am glad I haven't got any father to bother me like that! I never had any trouble about my relations," laughed Noddy.

"You must not talk so, Noddy; it does not sound well. If you had a good and kind father, as I have, he would be a great joy to you."

"But your father don't seem to be a great joy to you just now," added Noddy, whose philosophy had been developed at the expense of his affections.

"Yes, he is; and even if I knew that he were dead"—and Bertha shuddered as she uttered the words—"the remembrance of his love and kindness would still be a great joy to me."

"Well, I don't understand those things, and I suppose I ought not to say anything about them," said Noddy, as he observed the great tear that slid down the pale cheek of Bertha. "There's going to be a race today."

"What kind of a race?"

"Mr. Richard is going to race with Tom Mullen. Each one put up five dollars, and Bob Bleeker has got the money."

Bertha was shocked at this piece of news, for it assured her that her brother had never made a resolution to abandon his evil associates, or that he had broken it.

"Are you sure of what you say, Noddy?"

"Yes; I am certain of it. Tom Mullen told me all about it yesterday."

"Where did you see him?"

"I saw him on the river. You know you lent me your boat to go up to the island, and I met him on my way back. The reason why he told me was, that he wanted to know what Mr. Richard had been doing to his boat, to make her sail faster."

The conversation was interrupted by the ringing of the breakfast bell. Bertha noticed that Richard was more than usually excited. He hurried through the morning meal, and hastened down to the wharf, whither Bertha followed him, and joined him on board the *Greyhound*.

"I wish you would take the morning train to the city, Richard, and ascertain what has become of father," said Bertha, as she stepped into the sailboat. "I feel almost sure something has happened to him."

"I can't go today," replied Richard, impatiently.

"Why not, Dick?"

"Because I can't. I think that is reason enough."

"How rude you are! If you felt as badly as I do, you would be glad to go."

"Badly? Why should you feel badly? Don't you think father is old enough, and knows enough, to take care of himself?"

"You know he has the heart complaint, and—"

Bertha could not complete her sentence, for there was in her mind a vivid picture of her father lying dead in his office, where he might have fallen when there was no one near to help him, or even to witness his expiring agony. She burst into tears and wept in silence, with the awful picture still before her mental vision. Richard, disturbed by none of his sister's doubts or fears, coolly cast loose the sails of the *Greyhound*, and made his preparations for the exciting event of the day. Bertha continued to weep, without his sympathy or even his notice, for a time.

"My poor father!" sobbed Bertha.

"What are you crying about, Berty?"

"I am almost certain that something has happened to father. He never stayed away overnight before without letting us know where he was."

"Oh, nonsense! He is full of business, and something has detained him. If he were sick, or anything worse had happened to him, we should have heard of it before this time. I tell you it is all right."

"Even if it is all right, it will do no harm to ascertain the fact. You can go to the city this morning, and return by the noon train," said Bertha, whose anxiety for her father had overshadowed everything else, and even made her forget the race of which Noddy had told her.

"I told you I couldn't go this morning," answered he, petulantly. "Why don't you go yourself?"

"I cannot leave today. Fanny is to have her party this afternoon."

"Well, I can't go, and it is of no use to talk about it. I have an engagement that I must keep."

"I hope you are not going with that wicked Tom Mullen again," added she, as Noddy's unpleasant intelligence recurred to her mind.

"I don't want any preaching."

"You are going with those boys again! Oh, Richard! I beg of you, do not."

"What's the matter now?" sneered Richard.

"Stay at home today with me, Richard. You don't know how lonely and sad I feel."

"The more fool you!"

"How unkind you are, Dick!"

"Come, Berty, don't whine any more; that's a good girl," said he, changing his tone as policy, rather than feeling, seemed to dictate. "If father doesn't come home before three o'clock, and you don't hear from him, I will agree to go to the city by the afternoon train, and find out where he is. Positively, Berty, that is the best I can do. Now, be a good girl, Berty, and go ashore, or you won't be ready for Fanny's party."

"I feel almost as bad for you as I do for father," sobbed Bertha.

"Why, what under the canopy of Jupiter has got into you now?" exclaimed Richard, suspending his work, and looking in her face with astonishment.

"I know you are going to do something wrong today, Dick."

"Do you, indeed? Then you are a long way ahead of my time. What do you mean?"

"You are going to sail your boat against Tom Mullen's."

"Who told you that?"

"Isn't it so, Dick?"

"Well, suppose it is; what then? There is no great harm in racing boats, I hope."

"And you have put up five dollars, as a bet, on the race."

"Who told you this?"

"Is it true, Dick?"

"Perhaps it is, and perhaps it isn't; what then?"

"You don't answer me, Dick!"

"Did you ever hear of such a thing as a race for nothing?" answered he, sullenly. "I would give another five dollars to know who told you this."

"Money seems to be very plenty with you, though father hasn't given you any for six or seven weeks."

"Now, you have said enough, Berty, and you may go ashore. Do you think I am going to listen to your preaching, and have you domineer over me, like that? If you don't leave the boat, I will help you ashore," said Richard, who was now so angry that he had lost control of himself.

"Don't be angry, Richard. You are my brother and you know I would not willingly offend you."

"That's just what you are doing."

"But you are going with those bad boys again. You are taking your first steps in gambling. If you knew how bad these things make me feel, you wouldn't be cross to me. I don't want to have my brother like Tom Mullen."

"Now, shut up! Don't whine any more over me. I am able to take care of myself, and I don't want a sermon from you every time you happen to have the blues."

"Where did you get the money, Dick, to bet on the race?"

"That's none of your business," replied Richard, rudely. "Do you mean to hint that I stole it?"

"I hope not, Dick."

"If you haven't any better opinion of me than that, you had better hold your tongue."

"You remember the other time, when you were going to have this race with Tom Mullen? You know what you were tempted to do that time?"

"That was father's money, and just as much mine as it was yours. You wouldn't lend me the money, and you see what you made me do."

"I only wanted to keep you away from those boys. If father were at home, you know he wouldn't let you go."

"He couldn't help himself," growled Richard; "and you can't; so you may as well go into the house, and hold your tongue."

"Won't you give up this race for my sake, Richard?" pleaded the poor girl, whose solicitude was now divided between her father and her brother.

"No, I won't! All the teasing, scolding, preaching, fretting and threatening in the world won't make me back out this time."

"At least tell me where you got the money that you put up."

"I won't do that, either," said Richard, stoutly. "I came honestly by it, and that's enough for you to know. You need not scold or threaten any more, but go home."

"I haven't threatened you," sighed Bertha; "you know I didn't tell father about the ten dollars."

"I know you didn't; but you told him I went with Tom Mullen and the rest of the fellows, and that was just as bad."

"I did it for your good."

"If you won't go ashore, I will!" said Richard, angrily, as he jumped into his skiff and paddled to the wharf as fast as he could.

Poor Bertha, trembling for her father and her brother, was sorely tried by the unfeeling conduct of the latter. She could do nothing to restore the one or redeem the other. Richard would go, though she had done all she could to prevent him from doing so. As she sat weeping in the boat, she tried to think of some plan to keep Richard at home. She knew that Ben could do it; that he would even lock him up in the boathouse, if she wished him to do so; but she was unwilling to resort to extreme measures.

Whatever else might be, it was certain that crying would do no good; and summoning all her resolution, she dried her tears, and determined to make the best of her trying situation. Stepping into the boat, she rowed to the shore. Her resolution was already imparting new courage to her soul, and she felt that she could endure all that might be in store for her. But she did not abandon her purpose to save her brother. He had left her in anger, and she hoped, when he became himself again, that he would hear her.

As she passed up the path toward the house, where Richard had gone, she saw Ben hastening toward her with all the speed his rheumatic joints would permit. As he approached he held up a letter, which caused Bertha's heart to beat with hope and fear.

"Here is a letter, Miss Bertha. The handwriting is your father's; so I suppose nothing has happened to him," said Ben, as he gave her the letter.

"I hope not. Where did you get it?" asked Bertha, as she tore open the envelope.

"The conductor on the morning train brought it up."

Bertha's face lighted up with pleasure as she read the first line; but as she proceeded with the letter, her expression changed, and the shade of sadness deepened into a look of grief and alarm. The letter was as follows:

New York City,
August 12th.

My Dear Children:

An unexpected event detained me in the city last night, and prevented me from sending you any word that I could not go home as usual; but I am alive and well, and I hope my unexplained absence did not cause you any anxiety or alarm.

"But, my dear children, the event to which I allude promises the most serious consequences to me in my business relations, and before many days you may be called upon to share with me the trials and misfortunes from which only a few men in active business life can be exempted. You may be compelled to give up the comforts and luxuries of our elegant home; but while your father retains his honor and integrity, can you not bear with him the loss of everything else? I do not yet know the extent of my misfortune, and I have only mentioned it that you might the sooner learn to endure with patience the change to which we must submit.

"I shall not be able to go home tonight or tomorrow night—perhaps not for several days. I am much distressed by the aspect of my business affairs; but it would be a great relief to me, when I do go home, to find that my children have the courage to endure the heavy blow that has come upon us. Be patient and hopeful, and all will yet be well with us.

Your affectionate father,

Franklin Grant

Bertha was astonished and bewildered by the contents of this letter. She told the boatman that her father was alive and well; but she deemed it prudent to conceal the rest of the letter from him for the present. The bad news it contained would travel fast enough, without any assistance from her.

While reading the letter, she had seen Richard come out of the house and walk off in another direction. She asked Ben to find him, and send him to the house, where she went herself, rejoiced to find her worst fears were not realized, but almost stunned by the shock which the letter had given her. It was terrible to think of leaving Woodville; to step down from the pinnacle of wealth to the low level of poverty; but, as she had been rich and humble, the fall would be a gentle one to her; yet how terrible to Richard and Fanny!

Richard read the letter, turned pale, and wondered what it all meant. Bertha said it was plain that her father had failed in business. She was calm and resigned, he was morose and sullen.

"You will not go to the race now, Dick?" she asked.

"I will!" and he rushed out of the house, down the hill, to the wharf; but when he got there, nothing but the topmast of the *Greyhound* could be seen.

She had sunk in fifteen feet of water!

CHAPTER 6

THE "GREYHOUND" FLOATS AGAIN

The rage of Richard knew no bounds when he discovered the topmast of the *Greyhound*, with the little tri-colored flag still flaunting upon it, rising but a few feet above the waves of the Hudson. There she had floated, as gayly and as buoyantly as a swan, only an hour before. But there was no one near to hear his exclamations of wrath and disappointment, as he beheld the ruin of all his hopes for that day. I am sorry to add that he swore roundly; but a boy who could associate with rowdies and blacklegs would not be too nice to use profane language.

While he was still venting his impotent frenzy, Ben arrived at the wharf. The boatman had not discovered the calamity which had befallen the *Greyhound* till he reached the wharf, for the gloomy expression of Bertha still haunted his mind, and he was wondering what had happened to cover with shadows the face which was wont to be all sunshine. When he raised his eyes from the ground, and looked off upon the water—as an old sailor always does when he first comes near the sea, or on deck from below—he saw the flaunting flag of the *Greyhound*, fifteen feet lower down than when he had last looked upon it, and he appeared to be quite as much surprised as Richard.

"Ben, who did that?" roared Richard, as the boatman moved out to the end of the wharf.

He was almost bursting with anger and vexation; and no doubt his mind was filled with suspicions and conjectures in regard to the author of this mischief, for he had already come to the conclusion that it had an author, as the *Greyhound* would never have done so mean a thing as to sink without assistance.

Ben was an elderly man, and he had always been treated with consideration and respect by Mr. Grant and all his household; therefore he felt that the tone with which "Mr. Richard" addressed him was not proper or even tolerable.

"I don't know, Mr. Richard," replied the boatman, in a gruff, man-of-war tone, and without even condescending to express any regret or surprise at the singular event.

"If I knew who did it, I would kill him!" foamed Richard.

"Then it is lucky for him that you don't know," added Ben, rather coolly.

"She didn't sink herself."

"I didn't say she did, Mr. Richard."

"Then who did it?"

"I don't know."

"Yes, you do know; and if you don't tell me, I'll hold you responsible for it," said Richard with an emphasis which ought to have produced a startling effect upon the old boatman.

But it did not appear to produce any effect; for Ben hitched up his long blue trousers, turned upon his heel, and slowly walked off.

"Why don't you answer me, Ben?"

"I haven't anything to say, Mr. Richard," replied the old man, continuing his walk up the wharf.

"How dare you turn your back upon me in that manner? Come back here, and answer my questions."

As Ben would not come back, Richard went to him, and, with clinched fists, placed himself in front of the old boatman, as though he meant to thrash him on the spot for his impudence. If Richard had been himself, as his hump-backed namesake declared he was on a certain occasion, he would not have ventured into this belligerent attitude. He was beside himself with passion, and there was neither wisdom nor discretion left in him.

"Mr. Richard," said the boatman, after he had deliberately surveyed the youngster from head to foot for a moment, "you are my employer's son, and I don't want to harm you; but I don't allow anyone to insult me. I am a poor man, but there isn't anybody in the world that is rich enough to insult me. Now, get out of my way."

"Tell me who sunk that boat!"

The great, broad hand of the old boatman suddenly dropped upon the shoulder of the youngster, a vigorous shaking followed, and he was laid upon the ground as gently as a mother would deposit her babe in the cradle. That strong arm was too much for Richard, and when he rose, he placed a respectful distance between himself and the owner of it.

"You did it! I know you did!" growled Richard. "I will pay you for it before you are many days older."

Ben deigned no reply to this rude speech, but walked up the lawn toward the house. On his way he was met by Bertha, who from her window had discovered the mishap which had befallen the *Greyhound*, as well as witnessed the scene we have just described; and she was coming down to make peace between the parties.

In a few words Ben told her what had happened, assuring her that he was entirely ignorant of the cause of the sinking of the boat.

"Mr. Richard is very angry just now, and I think you had better keep away from him for a time. When he comes to himself, he and I have an account to be squared," said Ben.

"Don't be angry with him. He will be sorry for what he has done."

"Bless you, Miss Bertha, I'm not angry. I couldn't get angry with a youngster like him if I tried," added the boatman with a benign smile.

"I hope not."

"Mr. Richard is a good-hearted boy, and before he began to run with those beggarly rowdies on the other side, he was an honest and well-meaning boy. If I had him on board ship, a thousand miles from the nearest land, I could make a man of him in three days."

With this encouraging remark, Ben hitched up his trousers again, and continued his walk toward the house. Acting upon the suggestion of the boatman, Bertha decided to let her brother cool off for a while, before she went near him. The sinking of the boat seemed like a providential event to her, since it must prevent the race she so much dreaded. Yet if Richard had the will to associate with dissolute persons, even this accident could not restrain him.

She could not help asking herself, as she sat waiting for Richard's wrath to subside, what effect the change of fortune would have upon him. If it saved him from the error of his ways, it would be a blessing instead of a misfortune. Her brother was proud, and gloried in the wealth and social position of his father. The rowdies of Whitestone had discovered his weak point, and as long as he paid for the oysters, cigars—and liquors, for aught we know—they were willing to flatter him, and to yield the homage which he so much coveted.

Misfortune had swept away the wealth of his father, and he was placed on a level with those who had before looked up to him. If Mr. Grant had the will, he had no longer the ability to furnish his children with money, as he had done before. But Richard still had a large portion of the fifty dollars left, and he was not disposed to consider any of these questions. They did not even occur to him. His mind was all absorbed by the race.

When she thought a sufficient time had elapsed for Richard to recover his self-possession, Bertha joined him on the wharf, where he still sat, brooding over the ruin of his hopes. He noticed Bertha as she approached, but his interview with Ben had evaporated the violence of his temper, and he permitted her to seat herself by his side without uttering a word.

"Richard, I am sorry you were so rude to Ben. He is an old man, and he has always been very kind to you," said Bertha in the gentlest tones of peace and affection.

"He had no business to sink my boat then," muttered Richard.

"He did not do it."

"How do you know he didn't?"

"He went down to the railroad station while we were at breakfast, and did not return till after you came on shore. He handed me the letter as I was going up to the house, and then went for his breakfast. He did not come down here again until after you did, and then he found you here. It is impossible that he should have done it."

"Then you must have done it yourself."

"No, Richard; I did not. You have had your eyes upon me ever since we landed from the boat."

"You knew about the race, and wanted to prevent me from going to it."

"But I did not sink your boat; neither do I know by whom it was done."

Richard knew that Bertha always spoke the truth, and he would as soon have doubted his own existence as doubted her word. In spite of his theory that she had done it, or caused it to be done, to defeat his plans, he was compelled to believe what she said.

"I don't understand it, then," said he, greatly perplexed. "You were the last person on board of her."

"It is as much a mystery to me as it is to you; but I hope you will give up this race."

"I can't do anything else now. I put the money up, and I suppose I have lost it."

"That is of little consequence."

"So you say; but the fellows will think I did it to avoid the race."

"Let them think so; it won't injure you."

"But I would give a good deal to know how it was done."

"Perhaps some boat ran into her while she lay at her moorings. How do you know that Tom Mullen didn't do it?"

"He wouldn't do such a thing."

"He isn't any too good to do a mean action."

"If I thought he did do it!" said Richard, as he jumped from the seat, apparently convinced that he did do it. "Where is Ben? I wonder if we can't raise her, and have the race yet?"

"Do you think Ben would help you now?" asked Bertha, reproachfully.

"I am sorry for what I said to him; but I was fully convinced that he had done the mischief by your order. I will beg his pardon;" and Richard ran up to the house, and made his peace with Ben, which was not a difficult matter, for the old boatman was almost a grandfather to all three of the children.

"Certainly, Mr. Richard, I forgive you with all my heart, and I am glad of the chance to do so, for this thing made me feel worse than it did you. Now we will go down and find out what made the *Greyhound* go to the bottom," said Ben, as he led the way to the wharf.

Bertha had returned to the house, to attend to the preparations for Fanny's party, or possibly she might have objected to any investigations in the direction indicated. Richard did not have the courage to ask Ben to help raise the boat; but when they reached the wharf, the old man went to the boathouse, and brought out sundry coils of rigging, blocks and other gear. Then, with the end of a line in his hand, he stepped into Bertha's boat with Richard, and sculled off to the place where the *Greyhound* had sunk.

Fastening the line to the painter of the sunken boat, he sculled back again. On their return to the wharf, they found Noddy there, an anxious observer of their proceedings.

"Noddy, do you know who sunk this boat?" said Richard, who happened to think just then that the little savage had been sitting on the pier during the angry interview between himself and Bertha.

"I expect she sunk herself," replied he, with one of his wild leers.

"If you know anything about it, tell me at once," added Richard, sternly.

"I don't know anything about it."

"Yes, you do, you little villain!" continued Richard, beginning to get excited.

"Keep cool, Mr. Richard," interposed the boatman. "We have no time to spare in that manner. Of course the boy don't know anything about it. Here, you young sculpin, run up and tell John to bring the two plow horses down here as quick as he can."

Noddy, whose health was now almost restored, ran off toward the stables, chuckling as he went, as if he was glad to escape any further questions.

Ben now sent Richard up into a large tree which grew on the very verge of the water, where, under the old man's directions, he fastened a block, and passed the long line from the boat through it. Another block was attached near the ground, and the line run through it. By this time the horses had come, and were hitched to the end of the rope.

Richard was deeply interested in the operation, and what he could not understand, the boatman explained to him. The rope was run through the block in the tree so as to pull the boat upward from the bottom of the river.

"Now start up the horses, John, very slowly, and stop quick, when I give the order," said Ben, as he stepped into the skiff, and paddled out to the mast of the *Greyhound*. "Now, go ahead, John," shouted he.

The horses pulled, and in a few moments the sailboat was safely landed on the grass by the side of the water. On examination, it was found that the plug in the bottom had been taken out, and greater than ever was the mystery in regard to the author of the mischief; but Richard, elated at the success of the boatman's labors, had ceased to care who had sunk the boat, so intent was he upon the prospects of the race.

The boat was baled out, and washed out, and half an hour of sunshine restored her to her former condition.

"Ben, I am ever so much obliged to you for what you have done, and all the more sorry for what happened this morning," said Richard, as the boatman was leaving the *Greyhound*. "You have saved me from disgrace and defeat."

"Why so?"

"I am going to run the race with Tom Mullen this morning."

"Are you? If I had known it, I wouldn't have raised your boat to save her from destruction," replied Ben, with a sad look.

"Miss Bertha don't want him to go," added Noddy, who was seated in the bow of Ben's boat. "I heard her teasing him to give it up, and he wouldn't."

"Shut up, you young monkey!" said Ben. "Boys should be seen, and not heard."

The old boatman used all the powers of his rude eloquence to dissuade Richard from going; but the latter prated about his faith and his honor, and declared that he must go; and he did go.

"Poor boy!" sighed Ben. "He is a smart, likely, good-hearted fellow, and it is a pity that he should go to ruin."

"Miss Bertha cried as though her heart would break, trying to make him give up the race. Something awful has happened to Mr. Grant, too," added Noddy. "I heard Miss Bertha say he had failed, if you know what that means—I don't."

"Failed!" gasped old Ben.

"Yes, sir; but Richard would go, and that's the reason why I pulled the plug out, and sank the boat," continued Noddy, innocently.

CHAPTER 7

TERRIBLE NEWS

Noddy Newman's confession promised to get him into trouble with Richard, if the latter should discover that he was the cause of the mischief. Ben, the old boatman, fully sympathized with the young savage in what he had

done; for, when the latter related the conversation between Bertha and her brother, to which he had listened, and told how badly he felt when Mr. Richard scolded at her, and declared that he would go to the race, his indignation was as deeply roused as that of the listener had been, and he decided that it would be better for all parties if the truth were concealed.

Richard had gone to the race, and there was nothing more that could be done to save him from the consequences of his own folly and waywardness. Noddy was well satisfied with what he had done, especially after the approval of Ben. All he lived for was to please Miss Bertha, and, if he could do anything to carry out her views, he was not very particular to avoid displeasing anybody else. If she wished to prevent Richard from going to the race, he was ready to sink the boat, or even to burn and destroy it. What the owner of her liked or disliked was a matter of no consequence to him.

Noddy's ideas of right and wrong, of truth and justice, were not very clearly defined. He had no particular devotion to the truth as such, and no particular love of justice for its own sake. He did not remain at Woodville because he liked the place, after he had strength enough to return to his former vagabond life, but because Bertha was there. He was willing to do right, so far as he understood it, because she desired him to do so. It must be confessed that principle had not yet been developed in his character. His only law was to do what his fair and loving mistress wished him to do, and he had no higher idea of duty than this. He cared for no one, was afraid of no one. Her friends were his friends, and, if she had had any foes, they would have been his foes.

Ben sat on the wharf, watching the *Greyhound*, as she swept forward on her course. He was sad and dull, for the information which Noddy had given him was full of grief to the old servant of the family. As he reflected upon the import of the fearful words which expressed the misfortune of Mr. Grant, the tears gathered on his brown cheek.

"What ails you, Ben?" asked Noddy, who was lying upon the wharf, gazing into the face of the boatman.

"What ails me? You young sculpin, are you here? I thought you had gone," replied Ben, roughly, as he wiped away the tears.

"You are crying!"

"Crying? Nonsense! Did you ever see an old sailor cry?"

"I never did before."

"I am not crying, you little lubber! I am getting old, and my eyes are weak. The sun makes them water a little."

"Tell me what it is about, Ben, and perhaps I will cry, too," added Noddy, suddenly dropping his chin, and looking as gloomy as though he had lost his best friend.

"Run away, boy—up to the house. Miss Bertha wants you to help her about the party. You must turn somersets, stand on your head, and cut all the capers you can this afternoon, to please the children who will come to the party, for I think it will be the last party the young folks will ever have at Woodville. Go and limber up your back, boy."

"I will do anything Miss Bertha wants me to do, if it is to swallow my own head, or turn inside out," replied Noddy, as he walked away, with the feeling that there was a chance for him to do something to please his young mistress.

On the way up to the house, he stopped in the grove to practice a few gymnastic feats, for he was not certain whether his ribs were yet in condition to enable him to entertain a party of young ladies. But his bones were all right, and his gyrations would have been creditable to a traveling circus company. When he had satisfied himself that he was in condition to perform, he walked leisurely up to the house to report to Bertha.

She did not give him much encouragement that his entertainment would be an acceptable one to the delicate young ladies who were to come from the homes of wealth and taste in the vicinity; but she was pleased with his devotion—with his efforts to do something for the amusement of the party. During the rest of the forenoon she kept him busy in preparing the rooms for the reception of the company, and Noddy was never so well satisfied as when he felt that he was doing something to assist or amuse Bertha.

At two o'clock in the afternoon everything was ready for the party. Miss Fanny was dressed like a fairy queen; Bertha, more plainly robed, was not less fascinating, and even Noddy Newman was so disguised by his new clothes that he looked very much like a little gentleman. Two o'clock came, and half-past two, and three, but not a single young lady who had been invited to the party made her appearance.

Fanny fretted, pouted and stormed at this want of punctuality, and even Bertha did not know what to make of it. But when four o'clock came, and still not a single guest appeared, Fanny gave up to despair, and Bertha was as puzzled as though she had been solving problems in Euclid. Five o'clock, and six o'clock, came, and still the great parlor of Woodville, with all its flowers and draperies, was "like some banquet hall deserted." Not a single guest came to the party of Miss Fanny, and the rich feast that decked the table in the great dining-room was "wasting its sweetness on the desert air."

Great were the astonishment and mortification of all in the house. Fanny had gone to her chamber, thrown off her fine clothes, and was weeping great tears of grief and vexation. The steward and the housekeeper were vainly trying to explain the circumstance. It was very remarkable.

"It is very singular," said Mrs. Green, "and such a slight was never put upon this family before."

"I can't understand it," added the steward.

"Neither can I."

"I can," said Noddy, thrusting his hands down to the bottom of the pockets in his new pants.

"You! What do you know about it?" said the steward.

"I think there must have been some mistake in the invitations," continued the housekeeper.

"I tell you, I know all about it," said Noddy.

"What do you know?"

"Mr. Grant has failed, and the people round here don't want to have anything more to do with him."

Neither the steward nor the housekeeper had heard anything of this kind before, and they were incredulous; but, Bertha, to whom Mrs. Green carried this piece of information, confirmed it.

"That is no reason why people should keep their children from coming to Fanny's party. Two or three of our neighbors have failed, and people sympathized with them, instead of insulting them, in their misfortune," said Bertha.

The failure of Mr. Grant certainly was not enough to explain the singular unanimity with which the guests of the party stayed away. The steward and the housekeeper were more indignant than before, and declared that they lived in the midst of the heathen. The cakes and the creams, the fruits and the candies, for the feast, were put away, the parlor was restored to its wonted condition; but grief, chagrin and indignation pervaded every hall and apartment at Woodville for the slight that had been put upon the family.

The hour for the return of Mr. Grant had arrived, and a man had been sent down to the railroad station to drive him up, as usual, for Bertha hoped that he might come that night, in spite of what he had said in his note. But the man returned alone, bringing the mail and the city newspapers.

As there was no letter from her father, Bertha took up one of the papers. The excitement of the party had passed away, and the all-engrossing theme of her father's misfortune once more began to prey upon her mind. Richard had not yet returned from the race, and she had a sad thought for him. Fanny and the housekeeper were discussing the party still, and Bertha tried to read the newspaper. She ran her eyes up and down the columns, in search of any item or article that might interest her.

Suddenly her gaze was fixed upon a paragraph, which accidentally caught her eye. It chained her attention, while her cheeks paled, her eyes dilated and her lips quivered. She read it through, as though some terrible fascination attracted her to the words; then the paper dropped from her hands, a slight groan escaped her pallid lips, and she dropped senseless from her chair upon the floor.

Mrs. Green, alarmed at her fall, hastened to her assistance, and, with a strong arm, placed her upon a sofa. She saw that Bertha had only fainted, and immediately applied herself with all zeal to her restoration.

"What ails her?" asked Fanny, who was greatly terrified by the deathlike appearance of her sister.

"She has only fainted; she will get over it in a few minutes," replied Mrs. Green, as she dashed a tumbler of ice water in the patient's face.

"What made her faint?"

"Poor child! She is all worn out. She didn't sleep any last night, worrying because her father didn't come home; and I suppose this affair of the party has vexed and tormented her, as it has all the rest of us."

"It is enough to make anyone faint. I wonder I don't faint," added Miss Fanny, who, no doubt, thought she had more sorrows, just then, than all the rest of the world put together.

Mrs. Green labored diligently and skillfully for the restoration of Bertha, and in a very short time the poor girl opened her eyes, and gazed languidly around the room.

"My poor father!" sighed she, and she shuddered so that her whole frame shook with the paroxysm, as she uttered the words.

"Come, dear, don't take it so sorely to heart; your father will come back again."

"Oh, Mrs. Green!" sobbed Bertha, as she looked at the housekeeper, and her eyes filled with tears. "What will become of me?"

"Don't take on so, Bertha. You have no reason to feel so badly, even if your father has failed."

"Failed!" exclaimed Miss Fanny, to whom this intelligence now came for the first time.

To the proud little miss this was the most terrible thing that could happen, and Mrs. Green began to fear that she should have another patient on her hands, for Fanny began to cry and rave as though she was to be the only sufferer by her father's misfortune.

"Come, children, you will make yourselves sick, if you take on in this way. It may not be half as bad as you think it is."

"My poor father!" sighed Bertha.

"No more parties, no more fine dresses; the horses and carriages must be sold, and all the servants discharged!" added Fanny, who, though only eleven years of age, knew what a failure meant, and had read some novels from which she had obtained the romantic idea of bankruptcy.

"What will become of him?" said Bertha.

"What shall I do?" added Fanny. "No one thinks anything of poor people."

"Come, Bertha, you had better go up to your chamber and lie down. You are all beat out with this party, and last night," suggested Mrs. Green.

"Has Richard come home?"

"He has not."

"I wish he would come, Mrs. Green. I must go to the city by the first train tomorrow morning."

"By the first train? Why! what for?"

"I must see father," sighed she.

"You must be calm, Bertha. This violent taking on don't seem like you."

"You don't understand it, Mrs. Green," added Bertha, looking sadly at the housekeeper.

"Oh, yes, I do; I have known a hundred people to fail, and some of them did not sell a single horse, nor discharge a single servant, but lived on just the same as they did before they failed. It isn't such a terrible thing, after all."

"You don't understand it," groaned Bertha, her eyes filling with tears again.

"Why, yes, I do. Some folks fail on purpose, and make ever so much money by it. Don't cry about it."

"It is nothing of that kind that makes me feel so."

"What in the world is it, then?" asked the housekeeper, astonished and alarmed by the reply.

"I cannot tell you. Do not ask me. You will know too soon. But I will try to be calm, and not disturb you and others by my conduct."

"Bless you, child! You don't disturb me, but I feel as bad as you do. I hope nothing bad has happened?"

"I cannot answer you," replied Bertha, as she shuddered at the thought of the terrible thing she had read in the newspaper. "There, I will not cry any more."

She rose from the sofa, and summoned all her strength to her aid; she tried to recover her wonted self-possession, but the blow she had received was too heavy and too awful to be easily resisted. She picked up the newspaper from the floor, and put it in her pocket, that none of the family might read the terrible paragraph which had taken away her reason for the time.

In her own bosom she locked up the fearful truth. She had no one to whom she dared to impart it. The reason why none of the children had come to the party was painfully apparent to her. The neighbors had read that stunning paragraph, and Woodville was no place for their children to visit after such a revelation.

Poor Bertha tried to eat her supper, but she could not. The terrible secret was burning at her heart. She dared not utter it, lest the housekeeper and the steward, and even old Ben, should desert the family, as the neighbors had done. But Richard was her brother, and she must tell him. He was older than she was, and such a shock as this would electrify him.

The secret seemed to gnaw at her soul, and she felt the need of a friend comforter, and Richard was the only one to whom she could muster courage to reveal it. After rising from the supper table, where she had vainly tried to eat, she hastened down to the wharf, to meet her brother on his return. As she approached the pier, she saw the *Greyhound* coming around the island. In a few moments it was within hail of the wharf, when Bertha discovered, with intense alarm, that Richard was not at the helm.

The boat was steered by Tom Mullen; but, on its nearer approach, the poor girl perceived the form of her brother lying in the bottom. She uttered a scream of terror, for he appeared to be dead.

"Don't be frightened, miss," said Tom Mullen, as he brought the boat alongside the wharf.

"Is he dead?" gasped Bertha.

"Oh, no, Miss Grant. Nothing of the kind. He took one glass more than he can carry, and it threw him," laughed Tom.

Richard was intoxicated! It was scarcely better than dead!

CHAPTER 8

THE NEW OWNER OF WOODVILLE

Bertha was shocked and almost paralyzed when she realized the condition of her brother. It was dreadful to see a mere boy, only fifteen years of age, in a state of beastly intoxication, and that boy her only brother, he to whom she had looked for counsel and encouragement in this hour of bitter trial. All her hopes seemed to be dissipated by this greatest calamity, and despair to be her only resort.

Tom Mullen's coarseness—for he alluded to the condition of Richard as though it were a matter of no consequence—grated harshly upon her feelings, and in a low tone she begged Ben, who had now come to her assistance, to send him off. The boatman and Tom bore Richard to the seat upon the pier, and then the former thanked the rowdy for what he had done for Mr. Richard, and proposed to take him back to Whitestone in one of the rowboats. Tom assented to the arrangement, and, much to the relief of Bertha, he bade her good-night, and stepped into the boat, leaving her alone with the helpless boy.

"Too bad," sighed Ben. "Too bad for a fine boy like Mr. Richard to come home in such a situation as that."

"That's a fact, Ben. I told him he had got enough, and advised him not to take the last glass. I did all I could to keep him straight, so it is not my fault that he comes home drunk."

"If he had never seen you, and the rest of the boys on the other side of the river, he might have been a decent boy."

"That is talking pretty close to the point!" replied Tom Mullen, sourly.

"Perhaps it is. Mr. Richard is a smart boy, and worth a dozen of the rowdies he goes with."

"Maybe he is; but, if he don't want my company, I am sure I don't want his. I can get along as well without him as he can without me. He wanted to race boats with me, and he did, and lost the race. I am five dollars better off for the affair than before, it is true, but I paid for all the liquor he drank."

"Don't say any more, Tom Mullen, or you will tempt me to throw you into the river!"

"But don't you see I am not to blame?"

"Silence! You have led this poor boy into all sorts of iniquity, and, if I thought you knew any better, I would take it out of your bones!"

Tom Mullen was a boy of seventeen. His feelings were deeply injured by the plain speech of the old boatman, if a person of his stamp had feelings, and he was disposed to resent these home thrusts; but he knew old Ben well enough not to attempt anything of the kind at present, and laid up his revenge for a more convenient season.

Ben landed his dissolute passenger on the pier at Whitestone, and hastened back to comfort Bertha, and attend to the besotted youth. On his return, he found the poor girl weeping over her brother.

"This is terrible, Ben!" sobbed she. "To think that Richard should ever come to this!"

"It's awful to see a man drunk, and I think the angels must weep to see a boy in such a state."

"What shall we do? I don't want to expose him to all the servants in the house."

"Leave him to me, Miss Bertha. I will take good care of him, and not a soul shall see him till he is all right again. Go up to the house; go to bed, and sleep as though nothing had happened."

"Thank you, Ben; you are very kind to save my feelings, and Richard's, too, for he will hide his head with shame when he realizes what he has done."

"I hope he will; and, bad as this thing is, it may be all for the best. It may be the very thing he needs to open his eyes and reform his life."

Bertha tried to hope that what the old man said might prove true, but just then there seemed to be no stability in anything human, and she could not help feeling that Richard was ruined forever—that his life would be that of the miserable sot, and end in the drunkard's grave. So many terrible events had suddenly been hurled upon her that she had begun to give way to the sense of gloom and despondency which the dark clouds of human ill often induce.

With a repeated charge to Ben to see that Richard was well cared for, she bade him good-night, and slowly walked up toward the house. She went to her chamber, and her prayers that night were longer and more earnest than usual, but they gave her hope and strength, for "earth has no sorrow which Heaven cannot heal." Exhausted by her physical exertions, as well as by her mental struggles, she soon wept herself to sleep.

As soon as Bertha left the wharf, the boatman at once applied himself to the redeeming of his promise. Lifting the inebriated boy in his arms, he carried him to a shallow place by the bank of the river, and, having removed his clothing, he commenced a vigorous course of hydropathic treatment, which partially brought the patient to his senses. Richard thought is was rather rough, when he had so far recovered from his stupor to be able to comprehend his situation, and he begged the doctor to desist; but Ben persevered till he was satisfied he had done his work thoroughly. He then carefully rubbed him dry, and led him back to the boathouse, where he made a bed for him of sails and boat cushions. The patient was still too stupid to offer any objection, and dropped asleep almost as soon as he touched his bed. Ben slept by his side, faithful to the charge given him by his young mistress.

The next morning Richard had entirely recovered from his debauch, with the exception of a severe headache. The vigorous treatment of the old boat-man had, no doubt, been highly beneficial. At all events, he was sufficiently recovered to be heartily ashamed of himself, for he realized that he had been intoxicated, and had a faint recollection of the energetic operations of Ben. But I am sorry to add that his pride was more deeply wounded than his prin-ciple. He began to think of what people would say, rather than of the wrong he had done. The feeling that he had disgraced himself and his family, rather than sinned against God and himself, took possession of his mind.

He was soon called to a realizing sense of his conduct by the vigorous scolding which Ben gave him. The old man was as faithful in his admonition as though the boy had been his own son; and Richard's shame and mortifi-cation did not permit him to utter a word in his own defense. While he was undergoing this severe lecture, Bertha came down to inquire for his health. The boatman brought his address to an abrupt conclusion, and told Bertha what he had done, and that the patient was in as good condition as could be expected after such a time.

"Come up to the house with me, Richard," said Bertha; "I want to talk with you."

"I have had talk enough, and I don't think any more would do me any good," replied Richard; but the remonstrance was very tame, for him.

"I will not reproach you for what you have done, Dick. I will leave that to your own conscience. I have something else to say to you."

"I don't want to go up to the house, and be laughed at by all the ser-vants. I feel more like clearing out somewhere, and never seeing anybody that knows me again."

"No one at the house knows anything about your conduct."

Richard thought it was very considerate on the part of Ben and his sister to conceal his infirmity from others, and he felt grateful to them for sparing his pride. He walked up to the house with Bertha, and, after he had changed his clothes and eaten his breakfast, they met again in the library.

Just before breakfast Mrs. Green had told him about the failure of Fan-ny's party, and the fainting of Bertha. He was indignant at the slight upon the family, and pitied poor Bertha, who had taken it so sorely to heart. He reproached himself more than ever for his own conduct, and determined to make what reparation he could for it.

"I did not think our neighbors were so heartless before," said Richard, as he entered the library, where Bertha was waiting for him. "It makes my blood boil to think of it."

"I am not at all surprised at their conduct. Perhaps they kept their children at home from the best of motives, for they probably knew more of our affairs than we did ourselves," replied Bertha, as she wiped away the tears from her eyes, which would come in spite of all her efforts to repress them.

"What do you mean by that, Bertha?"

"Father is utterly ruined."

"Well, he has failed, I suppose; but I—"

"Or, worse than that—as much worse than that as can be!" exclaimed Bertha.

"Why, what has happened? You had a letter from him yesterday, saying that he was alive and well."

"I did; but he did not tell us the whole truth."

"Why, what do you mean, Bertha? What can have happened to him?"

"He is not only ruined, but he is in prison."

"In prison!" exclaimed Richard, shocked at these words.

"In the Tombs," replied she, covering her face with her hands. "I read it in the newspaper last night."

"What has he done?" demanded Richard, with quivering lip.

"He was arrested on the charge of fraud—the paper says stupendous frauds in his business. I do not understand it, but I am sure, very sure, that father has not done anything wrong. I know he would not do it."

"Certainly not," added Richard, biting his lip till the blood ran.

"The newspaper says that he was arrested in an attempt to leave the country, which rendered his guilt all the more apparent; but I do not believe it."

"Nor I," added Richard.

"Here is the paper; you can read the paragraph, and perhaps you will understand it better than I do," said Bertha, as she took the paper from her pocket.

Richard read the article, and then read it again; but the complicated transactions which it described were as much beyond his comprehension as they had been beyond his sister's. The failure of an extensive English banking house had been the beginning of Mr. Grant's misfortunes, and the alleged frauds were committed in attempting to sustain himself against the pressure caused by being deprived of his foreign resources. But, my young readers would be as much in the dark as Richard and Bertha if I should attempt to explain the situation of Mr. Grant's affairs. It is enough to say that all the apparent wealth of the broker, immense as it had appeared to himself and to his neighbors, had suddenly been swept away, and that he was thrown into prison on the charge of fraud.

Since the preceding evening Bertha had borne this heavy load upon her heart, made ten times heavier by the misconduct of her brother. The consciousness that she could do nothing to aid her father, or even to comfort him, was not the least of her troubles. Mr. Grant had concealed from his children the fact of his arrest and imprisonment, and she had given up her purpose to visit him in his prison, for it could only add to his grief, since he now supposed her to be ignorant of his real condition.

Among other items in the paragraph, the newspaper said that Mr. Grant had secured his principal and most pressing creditor by making over to him his splendid estate on the Hudson, with all its furniture, appointments, boats, library—indeed, everything there was at Woodville. This statement was even more startling to Richard than the fact of his father's arrest. All the worldly possessions of his father had passed away, almost in the twinkling of an eye. When he heard of the failure, he recalled the case of one of the neighbors, who, though a bankrupt, had retained his house and lands, and he had expected that his father would do the same. But now Woodville was gone; even the furniture in the house, the boats and the horses—all were to be given up, and the proud youth looked with disgust and contempt upon the poor cottage, or other humble abode, which his fancy pictured as the future residence of the family.

He was selfish, grossly selfish, in his pride and vanity, and he almost forgot the situation of his father in his mournings over the loss of the luxuries to which he had always been accustomed. Henceforth he was to be no better than the young men of Whitestone, who had regarded him with envy and admiration.

While he and Bertha were considering, from widely different points of view, the sad misfortune which had overtaken them, the man to whom Mr. Grant had transferred Woodville arrived to take possession of his property. As he was a money lender, and had no other god but his wealth, he was a hard man, rude and rough. Woodville would not pay him for the money he had lent its late owner, and obtaining possession of the place did not appease the anger which the failure of Mr. Grant had occasioned.

He was duly armed with all the necessary papers to make his work legal, and he had no regard for the feelings of the children or the servants. He walked all over the house and grounds, with his followers, and gave orders to the servants for the disposal of the boat and the horses.

"Can we remain here?" asked Bertha, in timid and trembling tones, as the new owner, for the third time, rudely entered the library, where Bertha and Richard were still seated, followed by all his train.

"How long do you want to stay?" demanded Mr. Grayle, the new proprietor, with an unfeeling stare at her and her brother.

"I don't know; till father comes home, I suppose," answered Bertha, alarmed and indignant at the coarse manner of the man.

"That will be a long time, I rather think," said Mr. Grayle. "Haven't you got any uncles, or aunts, or other friends, you could visit for a few weeks?"

"We have no relative but Uncle Obed, and he is in South America; but we will not stay here, if you do not wish us to do so."

"Well, I don't want to be hard with you. I have a purchaser in view, who will take the estate as it stands. He will be here tomorrow; but you can stay till I sell the place," said Grayle.

"Do you think he will buy it?" asked Richard.

"I am reasonably sure that he will."

"Then we must, indeed, leave Woodville," groaned Richard.

"I shouldn't think you would want to stay here, after what has happened," sneered Grayle. "But, if you want to stay, of course I shall not drive you out. As to your father's coming home, don't delude yourself on that point, young man. In my opinion, you won't see him for some years, unless you go where he happens to be."

"What do you mean by that?" demanded Richard, his face crimson with shame.

"I suppose you know where Sing Sing is? If you call at the penitentiary there, in the course of a month or two, you will probably find him."

"You are an unfeeling brute!" gasped Richard, filled with rage at the words and the sneers of the money lender.

"You are a little too bad," whispered one of the attendants of Grayle.

"I speak the truth. This young cub has been living at my expense for some time. He is prouder than his father, and it is time for him to open his eyes. But I won't be hard with them. I shall lock up the parlors, the library and the dining-room. They may have the use of the kitchen and their own chambers. We will send the servants off today. They may have their rooms and welcome, though I suppose they won't thank me for them," growled Grayle, as he left the library.

Richard and Bertha were almost stunned by these words; but they hastened from the library to their own chambers, to avoid further insult.

CHAPTER 9

BERTHA LEAVES WOODVILLE

There was no longer any room, if there was any desire, to conceal the misfortunes which had overtaken the owner of Woodville. The servants were all talking about the matter, and the astounding intelligence that Mr. Grant had been sent to the Tombs for fraud was spreading in every direction. Before night the steward and the housekeeper, the boatman and the grooms—indeed, all who had held any position at Woodville—were discharged. Not even Mrs. Green was allowed to remain, for Grayle feared that the affection of the late owner's employees might lead them to appropriate some of the property of their master. Perhaps his principal object was to drive the children from the place. Whether it was or not, it had this effect, for they could not remain any longer in the deserted home.

"What shall we do? We can't remain here any longer," said Richard, as the three lonely children met together in the chamber of Bertha. "There is not a servant left in the house. For one, I cannot remain here any longer."

"I feel that we are intruders; but where shall we go?" added Bertha.

"Anywhere—I care not where."

"But we have no place to go. Our rich and proud neighbors will not receive us now."

"If I knew they would, I wouldn't darken their doors," replied Richard, proudly.

"Nor I, after what they did yesterday," added Fanny.

"I cannot stay here, to be watched and dogged by that man whom Grayle has left in charge of the place. If I move, he follows me, as though he were afraid I would steal something," continued Richard, chafing under the new order of things. "I will not remain under this roof a single hour longer."

"Where shall we go?"

"We will go to the hotel over at Whitestone."

"To the hotel? How can we go to the hotel? We have not money enough to pay for a single day's board."

"Yes, we have. I have over thirty dollars in my pocket."

"Thirty dollars?" repeated Bertha, with an inquiring glance.

"Yes; thirty-five, I think."

"Oh, Richard!" sighed Bertha.

"Come, Berty, don't reprove me any more; and, as I have no longer any reason for keeping it secret, I will tell you that I had fifty dollars. I saved the man on the steamer from drowning, and gave him the name of John Green."

Bertha was not disposed to criticise his conduct at this time, but she was rejoiced to know that he had so much money, and that he came honestly by it. She readily assented to the plan of going to the hotel in Whitestone, and hastily packed up her own and Fanny's clothing in a trunk which belonged to her, as Richard had already done with his own wardrobe.

The trunks were carried downstairs by Richard and Bertha, and placed upon the piazza. They were heavy, and their weight reminded the proud youth of the condition to which he had fallen. He had never done such a thing as to carry his own trunk downstairs before. There were a dozen willing servants ready to do such work, but they had all been driven, like unclean beasts, from the premises.

But some of them had not gone far. Old Ben, like a guardian angel, hovered around the house, in spite of the orders of the keeper to leave; and no sooner were the trunks visible on the piazza than the boatman made his appearance. He had been up to Bertha's room several times during the day, and had done what he could to comfort her; but he was old and poor, and he had nothing to offer but words of hope and consolation.

"Are you going, Miss Bertha?" he asked, as the children came out of the house.

"Yes, Ben; we cannot stay here, where we are not wanted, any longer. We are going over to the hotel at Whitestone."

"Then I will go with you; and I am glad that you are going where I may have a chance to speak to you. These lubberly land sharks have been trying to drive me away from Woodville, but I shall not lose sight of the place while any of you remain. Dear me! This is the saddest day I ever knew in my life; but after a storm there's always a calm. Keep a cheery heart, and it will all come out right in the end," said Ben, as, with much difficulty, he shouldered the big trunk, and walked toward the wharf.

"Stop, there!" said a voice, in the direction of the stable.

At this moment Noddy Newman came bounding over the lawn, closely pursued by the keeper of the estate. The little savage had been driven off the premises a dozen times during the day, but he had as many times returned, determined not to desert Bertha in this hour of her extremity.

"Stop!" shouted the keeper. "Put down that trunk!" and the man placed himself in front of Ben, who, followed by Bertha and Richard, with the smaller trunk, was heading the little procession down to the pier.

"What do you want?" said Ben, gruffly, as he deposited the trunk upon the ground.

"I ordered you to leave these premises!"

"And I am going to leave them now, once and for all," replied Ben. "The children are going with me."

"You cannot carry off those trunks!"

"I think we can, if our strength holds out. Here, Noddy, take hold of that trunk with Mr. Richard."

"Stop, I say! You shall not carry those trunks off the place!"

"They contain nothing but our clothes," interposed Bertha.

"I don't know that," said the keeper, who was evidently a close imitator of his employer.

"I know it; go ahead, Ben," added Richard.

"I say you cannot carry off those trunks!" persisted the man.

"Can't we have our own clothes?" asked Bertha. "There is nothing else in them."

"Open them, and let me see!" added the man, roughly.

"I will not do it!" answered Richard, stoutly. "I give my word that they contain nothing but our clothing."

"What is your word good for, young man? You may open them, or carry them back to the house!"

"I will do neither! Move on, Ben."

Ben attempted to take up the trunk again, but the man put his hands upon it in such a manner as to prevent him from doing so.

"You miserable land shark!" said Ben, letting go the trunk. "You have all the law on your side, perhaps, but I have all the common sense and humanity on mine! Aren't you ashamed of yourself, to persecute these poor children in this manner?"

"I only do my duty," whined the keeper.

"I am going to take these things down to the pier, whether you are willing or not! I am ready to shake hands or fight with you; but I am going to do what I say!" and Ben proceeded once more to shoulder the trunk.

The keeper did not deem it prudent to interfere with him again, and perhaps he thought he was doing more than his duty required of him. The party reached the pier, and were on the point of putting the trunks into the four-oar barge, when the keeper again interposed, to prevent them from using the boat. This was plainly a part of Grayle's property, and there could be no question in regard to the man's right to interfere. He was inflexible, though Ben and Bertha both begged the use of the boat for a single hour.

Noddy stood by, watching, with intense interest, the proceedings, and so indignant that he could no longer contain himself. He began to abuse the keeper in round terms, and, finding this did him no damage, he picked up a large stone, and would have thrown it, if Bertha had not commanded him to drop it and be silent.

"Why don't you take the boat?" said he.

"Because it is not right to take it."

"Right! Humph!" pouted Noddy. "I would take it quick enough! But hold on a minute, Miss Bertha, and I will get you a boat," and away he ran down the bank of the river before she could stop him.

In half an hour he returned in a boat, with Bob Bleeker, whom he had hailed from the point below. Bob was what would be called a "rough" in the city of New York, but he was a man of generous heart, and had many good qualities. As his boat rounded up by the side of the wharf, he stepped ashore, and offered his services to convey the party over to Whitestone, for Noddy had already told him, with a good deal of coloring, about the conduct of the keeper.

He helped Ben put the trunks in the boat and then handed Bertha and Fanny to their seats. The keeper stood by, watching the movements of the party, and, when they were seated in the boat, and Bob was about to shove off, he uttered some insolent remarks.

"Stand by the boat hook a moment, Ben," said Bob, as he jumped on the wharf again.

"What do you want now?" said the keeper. "Be off—quick as you can!"

"I can't go till I have paid my respects to you!" replied Bob Bleeker. "You are the meanest Hottentot that ever landed on this side of North River! Couldn't you let these children have a boat to get out of your sight in?"

"Begone! None of your insolence here! I have got rid of them now!" growled the keeper.

"But you haven't got rid of me just yet! I want to leave you my card! There it is!" he added, striking the brutal wretch in the face with such force that the blow knocked him down. "I know how you've treated these children; I have heard all about it; and I couldn't leave you without something to remember me by. My name is Bob Bleeker, of Whitestone, and, if you want to meet me in a court of justice, I shall be willing to pay ten dollars or so for the sake of showing up such a villain as you are!"

The keeper picked himself up, and retreated from the spot, muttering vengeance upon the head of the chivalrous "rough."

Bob Bleeker did wrong to strike the keeper, however much the fellow deserved a whipping for his brutality. Noddy stood by, and witnessed the castigation, with a satisfaction that he expressed in the most extravagant manner. Bertha alone condemned the conduct of Bob; but she gave him credit for his good will.

The boat was pushed off, and in a few moments the fresh breeze carried them over to Whitestone. Bob and Ben conveyed the trunks up to the hotel, where they obtained two rooms. They were not such as the children had occupied at Woodville, but they were cheerful and comfortable. At an early hour Fanny, worn out by the exciting events of the day, retired to rest, leaving Richard and Bertha to consider some plan for the future.

Strange as it may seem, Bertha experienced a feeling of relief when she found herself domiciled at the hotel. She had left Woodville—had been almost driven from it; had been insulted and outraged in her feelings; but the tie which bound her to the home of her childhood had been snapped. There had been none of the sighs and tears with which she had expected to bid farewell to Woodville; she and her brother and sister had been too glad to get away from it. She felt stronger and more hopeful than she had since the first note of disaster had sounded in her ears.

However dark and forbidding the future might look, she was ready to meet it, for it seemed as though all of grief and misfortune that the world could have in store had already been hurled upon her afflicted family.

"What are we to do, Richard?" said she, as she joined him in his room.

"I don't know," replied he, blankly; "I have not thought of that yet."

"It is time to think of it."

"What can we do?"

"There are a hundred things that we can do. You are strong and healthy, and have been well educated. Perhaps you can find a place."

"A place? A place for what?" said Richard, looking curiously into the face of his sister.

"A place to work, of course," answered she, with no attempt to soften the words.

"A place to work!" repeated he, slowly, as if to obtain the full force of the idea. "What do you suppose I can do?"

"You can get a place to learn a trade, or you can go into a store."

"Get a place to learn a trade!" exclaimed Richard, rising suddenly from his chair, and walking up and down the room. "Don't you think the only son of Franklin Grant would look very pretty learning a trade? Don't mention such a thing as that to me again!"

"Why, Richard, I am surprised to find that experience has taught you nothing," replied Bertha. "You surely do not expect to be a gentleman, now that there is not a dollar of all your father's wealth left?"

"I intend to be a gentleman as long as I live."

"But you must work."

"I have money."

"Thirty-five dollars! How long do you suppose it will last? It will not pay our board for more than two or three weeks."

"Perhaps I can do something that is light and genteel. At any rate, I will see what can be done tomorrow; but I shall not learn any trade, I'll warrant you."

"You must conquer your pride, Richard, and remember that we are beggars now."

"Perhaps we are. I wonder when Uncle Obed is coming from Valparaiso? He is immensely rich."

"I don't know; we might starve before we heard from him."

"Starve? Pooh! What is the use of talking about such things!"

"We had better look things right in the face. I don't think you have considered our situation. We have neither money nor friends. We must work for a living, unless you are willing to go to the almshouse and live on charity. I am not, and I intend to go to work."

"What are you going to do, Berty?" asked he, with an incredulous smile.

"I don't know yet; I am going to work."

"Don't disgrace yourself and your family, Berty."

"What nonsense you talk, Richard! We are beggars and outcasts, and it is all folly to talk about disgracing myself or the family. I shall find something to do in a few days. I wish I could see father. He would tell me what to do."

Richard's pride could not yet be conquered, and Bertha retired, feeling that the rude hand of necessity would soon make hard terms with them. But, with such views as he held, it was not safe to remain at a hotel, and she resolved to find a cheaper residence the next day.

CHAPTER 10

BERTHA VISITS THE WIDOW LAMB

On the following morning Bertha, who, in spite of her cares and trials, had slept well, rose early, and applied herself, with zeal and energy, to the great work before her—a work so difficult and delicate that it would have challenged the whole ability of a mature and experienced mind. Her pathway was full of trials and perplexities, for she had but little knowledge of the world, and was without the aid of influential friends.

There were two very difficult problems, which required an immediate solution. The first was, what to do with Fanny; and the second, whether Richard would be a help or a hindrance to her. If there had been no one but herself to provide for, the task would have been an easy one. Fanny was too young to do anything for herself, and Richard's pride was a stumbling-block in his path. The thirty-five dollars in her brother's possession was but a small sum to pay the expenses of a family; but she was not sure that even this would be devoted to the purpose.

Her father was languishing in prison. He was suffering for himself and suffering for them, for she knew that his greatest grief would be the thought of his children, now cast, penniless and unprotected, upon the cold world. She wanted to do something for him, and she would gladly have gone to his prison, and shared its gloom and its horrors with him, if she could take the weight of one straw from the heavy burden he was compelled to bear. But the nearer and more pressing duties of the hour would not permit her to yield even this filial offering till she had done something to prepare for the cold and forbidding future.

These were some of the perplexities; but the perils and difficulties that surrounded her seemed to give her new strength and new courage. The words of the Scripture, "As thy day, so shall thy strength be," as embodied in a beautiful and comforting poem by Mrs. Sigourney, lingered encouragingly in her mind, to sweeten the cup of adversity and nerve her soul for the conflict of the day. On this morning, therefore, she was calm and resolute, and looked hopefully forward to what the day might bring forth.

Her first care was for Fanny, and she had already decided what disposition to make of her. She intended, with the assistance of Ben, to find a place in some poor but respectable family, where she could be boarded for a small sum. Bertha hoped that before many weeks the family might be united again under one roof, however humble; and this arrangement was to be only a temporary one.

While Richard and Fanny were still sleeping, she looked out of her window, and saw the old boatman walking up and down in front of the house. He had lodged with Bob Bleeker; but, very much as a faithful watchdog keeps guard over the property of his master, he kept his eyes upon the children, without being forward, or intruding upon them at unseemly hours. Bertha passed through the silent halls of the hotel and joined the boatman upon the piazza, where she informed him of her plan in regard to Fanny.

"Now, Ben, can you help me find a good place where she can be boarded for a small sum? For, you know, we cannot afford to pay much."

"I know a poor widow woman, with whom I used to board myself, years ago; but the place would not suit Miss Fanny. It wouldn't be stylish enough."

"No matter for that, Ben. It will come hard to her, but she must learn to live as poor folks live. Is she a good woman?"

"There isn't a better on the face of the earth. She took care of me when I was laid up with the rheumatism. Mrs. Lamb is a Christian woman, if there is one in this world," said Ben, with emphasis; "and, if I had a daughter, I don't know another person with whom I would more willingly trust her."

"Do you think Mrs. Lamb would be willing to take Fanny?"

"I think she would; only I am afraid Miss Fanny would give her a great deal of trouble. You know, she has very fine notions, and Mrs. Lamb's house isn't a bit like Woodville."

"Of course not; but Fanny may as well begin first as last to learn her lesson. I am sorry for her, poor child; I pity her, for I know it is a terrible blow to her to be deprived of the nice things she had at home."

"It is no worse for her than it is for you, Miss Bertha," added Ben, with a smile.

"I never cared so much for fine things as Richard and Fanny. It is no credit to me, for I suppose I was born so."

"Yes, Miss Bertha, one who has been rich and humble can be humble enough in poverty, but pride and want don't go well together."

"Where does Mrs. Lamb live?"

"About half a mile from here, just outside of the village. She has a very pretty cottage, which her husband left her when he died; but that is all she has, and she is obliged to work pretty hard for a living. She does washing and ironing for the rich people of the place, and she has as many friends as a member of congress. We will walk over to the widow's house, if you please, Miss Bertha. If you will walk along, I will follow you."

"Come with me, Ben," said Bertha, with a smile, as she took hold of his arm, and led him along for a few paces.

"I didn't know as you would like to walk with a rough-looking man like me," added Ben, as he dashed away a truant tear, which his pride and his affection had jointly contributed to form.

"I am not proud, Ben."

"You never were, Miss Bertha."

"What are you going to do, Ben? I have been so selfish that I have hardly thought of you."

"Oh, I shall do very well, Miss Bertha," answered Ben, with a smile of pleasure at this manifestation of interest on the part of his master's daughter.

"I had hoped you would always remain in our family; and it hurts my feelings to see you now, an old man, and rather infirm, thrown upon the world to take care of yourself."

"Don't think of me. I have my plans all formed."

"My father never gave you large wages, for I know he meant to take care of you as long as you lived. I suppose you haven't saved much?"

"Hardly anything, Miss Bertha. I sent all the money I could spare to my daughter, out West, after her husband died. I don't know how she will get along now. But I can manage to make some money. I have a matter of a hundred dollars or so salted down in the savings bank in Whitestone for a rainy day."

"That will not support you."

"No; I bargained for a boat, last night, with Bob Bleeker, and was to have given him this hundred dollars in part pay, but I—"

The old man suspended his speech at this point, and walked along, with his eyes fixed on the ground, while the long breaths he drew indicated the emotion that agitated his bosom.

"What, Ben?" gently asked Bertha.

"I didn't dare to pay away this money."

"Why not?"

"Since you were driven out of Woodville, I have thought this hundred dollars might be of some help to you."

"To me!" exclaimed Bertha. "I could not think of touching your money. Besides, we shall not need it. Richard has some money, and we shall get along very well. Keep it, Ben, for you will need it yourself."

"It is all at your service, Miss Bertha. It is little I can offer, but you are welcome to it."

"We shall not need it, Ben—really, we shall not."

"Then, perhaps, I had better buy the boat. I am going boating. There are plenty of people and parties in Whitestone who like to sail on the river; and, since Bob Bleeker gave up the business, there has been no regular boatman. I think I can do very well."

"I hope so, I am sure, Ben," replied Bertha, heartily. "I am rejoiced to find you have something to do that will suit your taste."

"I shall do very well, Miss Bertha. No one need worry about old Ben, as long as he has the use of his limbs. There is one thing more, Miss Bertha, which, I suppose, you have not thought about. What is to become of Noddy Newman?"

"Poor little fellow!" sighed Bertha. "I suppose I can do nothing more for him. Where is he now?"

"He slept with me at Bob Bleeker's last night. I suppose he will take to the woods, and become a vagabond again, if he can't stay with you. He don't seem to care for anybody on earth, Miss Bertha, but you, though he will mind me, for your sake. I believe the little fellow would die for you in a moment."

"Poor Noddy!" said Bertha. "I wish I could take care of him! He is a smart boy. I have taught him to read, and I had great hopes that I should make something of him."

"I have been thinking, Miss Bertha," added Ben, taking off his hat, and scratching his bald head, as though a magnificent idea had taken possession of his mind, "if you could induce the boy to stay with me, I will do as well by him as I can. I can read, and write, and cipher, and I will help him along with these things. He is smart and active, and having him with me in the boat would ease my old bones a great deal."

Bertha was delighted with this plan, and readily promised to do all she could to make Noddy stay with Ben. At this point in the conversation they arrived at the house of the Widow Lamb. The cottage, as the boatman had represented, was very neat, and even pretty, and Bertha thought her sister ought to be happy in such a place.

Mrs. Lamb was willing to take Fanny to board, for she was very fond of children, but Bertha frankly told her that the little miss might cause her a great deal of trouble, for she had been used to having a great many servants around her. The widow thought she could manage her; at any rate, she would try it, and she hoped she should be able to make her happy and contented. Bertha thought her price—two dollars a week—was very reasonable for one who was likely to be so difficult to please, and she took her leave of the laundress, agreeing to bring Fanny to her new home in the course of the day.

On their return to the hotel, Ben hastened back to Bob Bleeker's, to close the bargain for the boat, while Bertha went upstairs to announce the new arrangement to Fanny and Richard. The former had not yet risen, and as Bertha assisted in dressing her she told her what had been done.

"Then I am to live with a washerwoman!" said Miss Fanny, with a toss of her head.

"It is a very pretty cottage, and Mrs. Lamb is a very nice woman. You will be quite happy and contented there, if you are willing to be so anywhere that our small means will permit you to live."

"But only to think of it! Live with a washerwoman!"

"Fanny, we are all beggars now. We are poorer than Mrs. Lamb, with whom you will board. Beggars cannot be choosers, you know."

"Father will find me a better place than that."

"Father can do nothing for us now, if he ever can," replied Bertha, the tears filling her eyes. "He is in prison, and you ought to be thankful that you have a home at all."

The tears in the eyes of her sister touched the heart of Fanny. Her pride was the greatest defect of her character. She had never known much of a mother's care; if she had, she might have been a different person.

"What are you going to do, Bertha?" asked Fanny.

"I am going to work. I shall find a place where I can earn money enough to pay your board. I hope Richard will help me."

"Of course he will."

"Now, if you will go to your new place, and never complain of anything, nor cause Mrs. Lamb any trouble, you will do all I can expect of you."

"I will do the best I can."

"That is all I ask."

Bertha spent an hour in talking to her sister about her conduct in her new home; and Fanny, who seemed to be in a better frame of mind than ever before, listened attentively to all she said, and promised faithfully to conquer her pride and give Mrs. Lamb no trouble. She said she would wait upon herself, and never complain of her food or her apartment. Bertha regarded this as a triumph, for she felt that Fanny would try to do all she promised.

Richard turned up his nose at the idea of having his sister board with a washerwoman; but, as neither his figures nor his common sense would suggest a better plan, he was compelled to yield.

"Now, Richard, you must let me have some of your money, for, to guard against any accident, I wish to pay Fanny's board for two or three months in advance."

"I can't spare any money now. What's the use of paying her board before it is due?"

"We do not know what may happen. You and I can take care of ourselves and I think it is no more than right that we should provide for Fanny beyond the chance of an accident."

"But we must pay our own board."

"Of course, we cannot remain at this hotel."

"Certainly we can, at least for a time."

"What do you intend to do, Richard, for a living?"

"I don't know. I shall find something. How much money do you want?"

"You had better give me ten dollars. That will pay Fanny's board for five weeks."

"Ten dollars! Why, that is a third of all I have!" replied Richard, dismayed at the prospect of parting with so much of his funds.

Bertha had a double motive in asking for this large proportion of Richard's money. The first was to secure the payment of Fanny's board, in case her plans for the future should fail, and the second was that she had but little confidence in her brother's firmness. She feared that, while his money lasted, he would do nothing to help himself; that, while his pride had even thirty-five dollars for a foundation, he would spend his time in idleness, and perhaps do worse.

Actuated by these motives, she reasoned with him so forcibly and eloquently that he at last handed her the money, but he gave it up with a protest, and with many regrets. After breakfast the bill at the hotel was paid, and Fanny was taken to her new home. Bertha remained with her that day, putting her room and her wardrobe in order, and instructing her still further in the duties and relations of her new position.

Notwithstanding the odium of boarding with a washerwoman, Fanny liked the place very well and even thought she should be contented with Mrs. Lamb, who certainly did everything she could to smooth down the fall from the palace to the cottage.

During the day Ben and Noddy paid them a visit. The little savage seemed to take quite a sensible view of the new order of things, and when Bertha told him what had been done for him he agreed to remain with Ben, and be a good boy, if she would come and see him as often as she could.

Toward night Bertha returned to the hotel, where she found a letter from Richard.

CHAPTER 11

MASTER CHARLEY BYRON

Bertha was not a little startled when the clerk of the hotel handed her the letter, upon which she recognized the handwriting of her brother. It was ominous of disaster; at least, it suggested that Richard was not at hand to speak for himself, and she feared that his quick impulses had led him to take a step of which he had not, probably, considered the consequences. It required some courage to open a letter from him under such circumstances, and she held it in her hand for some moments before she could muster resolution enough to break the seal; and, when she did so, her worst fears were confirmed.

Richard wrote that he had been engaged by a gentleman to take his boat down to New York. He was to receive five dollars for the job, and, as it admitted of no delay, he had been obliged to sail at once, without seeing her. At the close of the epistle, Richard boasted a little of his first success in earning money, and declared that, when he got to the city, he should certainly find employment which would be both agreeable and profitable; and, when he did, he would inform her of the fact.

The thoughtless, impulsive boy had actually abandoned his sister, and, full of hope and conceit, had embarked in his career of life. Perhaps he thought Bertha was abundantly able to take care of herself, and did not need any assistance from him.

Bertha's doubts and fears were not for herself. She knew that Richard was thoughtless and flighty, and she trembled lest he should again fall into evil company. The city would have been a bad place for him, under any circumstances, but doubly so if he had no one to give him a friendly word of advice. He had gone, and, whatever she thought or felt in regard to him, nothing could be done to bring him back. She was now alone. The family had separated, and the path of each seemed to be in a different direction from that of the others.

She could not think of her situation without a feeling of sadness. A sense of loneliness, which she had not before experienced, came over her, which, with her anxiety for the fate of her father and her brother, had a very depressing influence upon her. But she had no time to indulge in sentimental emotions, for life had suddenly become real to her, and stern necessity compelled her to make it earnest.

As she had now disposed of Fanny, and Richard had disposed of himself, she had nothing to do but to apply herself to the remaining duty of the hour. She must go to work; but what to do, and where to find a place, were very perplexing questions. She was willing to do anything that she could, even to labor with her hands, if it would afford her the means of supporting herself and her sister.

With these thoughts in her mind, she walked through the principal street of Whitestone, to obtain any suggestion which the stores and other business places might give her. In her walks through the place, in more prosperous days, she had occasionally seen a notice posted in the windows of a "Saleswoman Wanted," or "A Young Lady to Act as Cashier." She walked up the street on one side and down on the other, attentively examining every window and door, in search of such a notice. But Whitestone, at the present time, did not need a saleswoman or a cashier. Disappointed and disheartened by her ill success, she walked down to the river, not from any motive, but because she had nowhere else to go.

Now for the first time since she had read her brother's letter, the thought came to her with fearful force that she had less than half a dollar in the world. This was not enough to pay for her lodging at the hotel, and she had not been to supper. Poverty seemed more terrible to her now than ever before. She began to feel that her situation was not only trying, but absolutely appalling. Even hunger and cold threatened to assail her, for the little money she had would not supply the necessities of life for even a single day. She could not dig, and she was ashamed to beg.

It was now growing dark, and she could not with safety remain in the streets any longer. There was only one house in the vicinity at which she believed she should be welcome, and this was the house of the Widow Lamb. It was revolting to her pride to force herself, as it were, upon a stranger; but she could not go to the hotel, and there was no other way to do. It was after the supper hour, and on her way through the village she stopped at a restaurant, and had a very simple supper of tea and bread and butter; but even this was purchased with a large part of all her worldly wealth.

Mrs. Lamb welcomed her to her humble cottage, and she passed the night with Fanny. But the future looked so blank and dismal to poor Bertha that she was less cheerful than usual, though she tried to conceal her doubts and fears from the widow and from her sister. Fanny had a thousand questions to ask, to only a few of which Bertha could give satisfactory answers.

"Have you got a place to work yet?" was asked a dozen times by the inquisitive little girl.

"I have not," answered Bertha, sadly; "and I am afraid I shall not be able to find one in Whitestone."

"What will you do?"

"I must go to the city, I suppose."

"Then you will see father."

"I shall certainly try to see him."

"You will tell him that I am a good girl—won't you?"

"I will, Fanny, and I am afraid that will be the best news I shall have for him."

"Tell him, too, that I am very sorry he is in prison, and I would do anything to get him out."

"I will, Fanny," replied Bertha, as she threw her arms around her neck and kissed her. "You have been a good girl today, and Mrs. Lamb says you have not only given her no trouble, but that you have helped her a great deal about her work."

"I tried to be good, Bertha," said Fanny. "I haven't complained a bit."

"I hope you never will."

"But I don't want you to go off and leave me."

"I must go, Fanny; but one of these days we shall meet again, and be all the happier for the trials and sorrow which we have been called upon to endure."

"I hope we shall," replied Fanny, whose conduct during the first day of her residence at the cottage had been very hopeful.

Fanny turned over and went to sleep after she had been duly praised and encouraged for her excellent demeanor. But Bertha's cup was too full to permit her to sleep. The morrow's sun promised to dawn upon a day of greater trial and difficulty than she had yet known. Twenty cents was all the money she had in the world, and Whitestone had no employment to give her. She must go to New York; but how to get there was beyond her comprehension. The distance was twenty-five miles, and she had not the means to pay her fare by railroad or steamboat.

The thought of borrowing a few dollars occurred to her; but there was no one, except the old boatman, of whom she would dare ask such a favor. Her pride—that self-respect which gives dignity and nobility to the character—revolted at the idea of asking even him for money, which she might never be able to pay. But while she was perplexed and agitated by these difficult problems, nature kindly came to her aid, and she dropped asleep without any plan for the coming day.

She was going to leave the cottage at an early hour the next morning, but Mrs. Lamb pressed her to remain until after breakfast; and then, with many tears, she bade farewell to her sister, not daring to believe that they would soon meet again. Bertha was stronger and more courageous than she had been on the preceding evening; for the more we look trials and troubles in the face, the more familiar we become with them and the less terrible do they seem to us.

With a feeling that she had only half done her work the night before, she again walked through the main street, and even had the hardihood to enter several of the larger stores and apply for a situation. Although she had no better success than before, she was strengthened by the consciousness that she had permitted no false pride to come between her and the attainment of her purpose. She had done all she could do in Whitestone, and it would be of no avail to remain there any longer.

Then came up the question again, how should she get to the city; for she had fully determined to go there. She could not walk, and she could not pay her fare. Why should she not walk, she asked herself. She was healthy and strong, and had always been accustomed to a great deal of outdoor exercise. There were no impossibilities to one in her situation, and whatever the result she would be no worse off on the way than if she remained in Whitestone. She decided at once to start, and leave the issue in the hands of that kind Providence which never permits the true and the good to be utterly cast down.

She would not think of leaving Whitestone without saying good-bye to Ben and Noddy; and for this purpose she went down to the wharf, where the boatman had the day before commenced business with his new boat. Much to her regret, she found they had gone up the river with a party of gentlemen, and would not return till late in the evening. Disappointed at this intelligence, she went to the hotel, where she had left her trunk, and wrote a short note to Ben, informing him of her intention. The clerk kindly promised to take care of her trunk till she sent for it, and she turned from the house to commence her weary pilgrimage.

Following the road near the bank of the river, she walked patiently and perseveringly for three hours, till she heard a clock on a church strike twelve. She was so faint and weary that she could walk no further, and seated herself under a tree by the side of the river to rest herself. She had retired a short distance from the road, so that she need not be subject to the rude gaze of those who passed.

In the last village through which she passed she had bought three small rolls; and upon these she made her dinner. A few blackberries that grew in the field were a great addition to the feast. Refreshed by her meal, and by an hour of rest, she resumed her walk. She had gone but a short distance before her attention was attracted by the loud cries of a child in a pasture adjoining the highway. The screams were so piteous that she could not help getting through the fence and hastening to the spot from whence they came, where she found a little boy, very prettily dressed, and evidently the child of wealthy parents, sitting on a stone. His eyes were red and swollen with weeping, and he was sobbing and moaning as though he had some real cause of grief. He was apparently about six years old. Bertha, moved by his distress, took him tenderly by the hand and gently patted his head, to assure him she was his friend.

"What is the matter, little boy?" she asked, when she had fully convinced him that she was not an evil spirit sent to torment him.

"I don't know the way home," blubbered the little fellow.

"Don't cry any more, and I think we can find your home. What is your name?"

"Charley."

"Haven't you got another name?"

"Charley Byron. I am six years old last May," replied Charley, suddenly brightening up and wiping away the great tears that still lingered on his cheek.

"You are a nice little fellow, and your education has not been neglected, I see."

"I can spell cat; c-a-t, cat," continued Charley, who appeared to have forgotten all his sorrows.

"You spelled it right," said Bertha, with a smile. "Do you know where your father lives?"

"My father lives in a great house on the hill; and I guess Mary'll catch it for letting me get lost."

"Where is Mary now?"

"I don't know where she is. She sat down on a rock and went to sleep. I was looking for blackberries, and when I wanted to find Mary again I couldn't. I have been walking ever so long, and I can't find Mary," said Charley, beginning to look very sad again.

"Don't cry any more, and I will help you find your father's house."

Bertha remembered that she had passed a large house on a hill, only a short distance back, and taking Charley's hand, she led him to the road.

It was a hard walk for little Charley, for he was so tired he could hardly move at all; but Bertha assisted him as much as she could, and at last they came to the gateway of the great house.

"That's my father's house," said Charley, just before they reached the gate.

"You can find your way now—can't you?" asked Bertha.

"Yes, but I want you to come up and see my mother."

"I think I will not go any further."

"Yes, but I want you to come up and see my mother; and you must come."

"I am very tired, Charley—almost as tired as you are—and I do not feel like walking up the hill."

"You can rest in my house."

"I think I will not go up, Charley."

"But you must come. I can't find the way if you don't," said Charley, tugging at Bertha's hand with a zeal which would permit no denial.

"If I must I must," said Bertha, yielding the point.

"I want to show you my new rocking-horse. Father sent it up yesterday, and it is a real nice one."

Charley led the way up to the front door of the house and pulled Bertha in after him. His mother, who had been terribly worried at his long absence, greeted him in the entry with a kiss, and asked him where the nurse was. Charley told his story in his childish way, and it was fully confirmed by the presence of Bertha, who was warmly welcomed by the grateful lady.

"Mary is growing very remiss of late, and I must discharge her," said Mrs. Byron, when they were seated in the sitting-room. "It isn't safe to trust Charley with her. The dear little fellow may get into the river. I have been worrying this half hour about him."

"He was crying bitterly when I found him," added Bertha.

"It was very good of you to take so much trouble."

"I couldn't leave him while he was so full of grief."

While they were talking the delinquent nurse arrived, very much alarmed at the sudden disappearance of her charge. But when she saw Charley she was greatly relieved, and invented a very plausible story to account for the accident. The story disproved itself, without any help from Charley or Bertha; and the result was that her mistress, provoked by her falsehood as much as by her neglect, promptly discharged her.

While Mrs. Byron was paying the girl, Charley exhibited his new rocking-horse and other treasures; but Bertha was absorbed by a new idea; she did not pay much attention to his prattle.

CHAPTER 12

BERTHA BECOMES A GOVERNESS

"There," said Mrs. Byron, as she joined her little son on the piazza, when the nurse had gone, "that is the fourth person I have had to take care of Charley. Now she is gone, and I don't know where I shall get another. It is not every person that I am willing to trust to take care of my little boy."

"It must be very trying to you," added Bertha, thoughtfully.

"I paid her ten dollars a month for her services; but I tremble to think of the dangers which Charley has escaped while in the care of these negligent servants."

"I suppose you would think I am too young to take care of Charley?" said Bertha, while her cheek crimsoned and her heart seemed to rise up into her throat.

"You!" exclaimed the lady, with a smile, as she glanced at Bertha from head to foot.

"Yes, madam; if you could give me twelve dollars a month, I should like to obtain the situation of governess of the child. I have had some experience in teaching children."

"You astonish me, miss. I do not even know your name yet."

"Bertha—" She was about to give her whole name but the thought suddenly occurred to her that, if she did so, her application would at once be rejected; and, without stopping to consider whether it was right or wrong to give a false name, she added: "Bertha Loring."

No sooner had she given this name than she regretted it; but conscious that she had no evil intention in doing so, she did not attempt to correct the error.

"Bertha Loring," added Mrs. Byron. "How old are you?"

"I am nearly fourteen."

"But you said you had had some experience in teaching children," said the lady, rather incredulously.

"Yes, ma'am. It was in a kind of mission school, and it was voluntary teaching."

"Ah, that, indeed," mused Mrs. Byron. "You are rather young, especially for the salary you ask."

"I have a sister who is dependent upon me for support, and I must do something by which I can earn about three dollars a week."

"Have you any testimonials of character or ability?"

"None, ma'am; I have never been in any situation yet."

"It would hardly be proper for me to place my only child in the care of a total stranger."

"Very true, ma'am," sighed Bertha; "but I have none."

"But I like your appearance and manners very much, and I am very grateful for what you have done for Charley. Perhaps you could refer me to some person with whom you are acquainted."

Bertha was about to mention the name of the clergyman in Whitestone, whose church her father's family had attended; but as the words were upon her lips, she happened to remember that she had not given her real name, and that the minister would not know any such person as Bertha Loring.

"For reasons which I could give, if necessary, I would rather not refer to any of my former friends," said Bertha.

"Your former friends?" repeated the lady, who, by this time had begun to obtain some idea of the circumstances of the applicant. "Are they not your friends now?"

"I do not know, ma'am," sighed Bertha. "As I have no references I think I will take my leave."

"Don't go yet, Miss Loring. I assure you I feel a deep interest in you, and only a necessary caution prevents me from engaging you at once. You must perceive that your situation is quite peculiar."

"Yes, ma'am, I know that it is; and therefore I am unwilling to trouble you any longer."

"You have evidently been well educated; and at your age you cannot possibly be an adventuress."

Bertha was not very clear what the lady meant by an adventuress, but she hastened to assure her she was not one.

"And I should suppose from your name that you belong to a good family."

"My father has been very unfortunate," replied Bertha, "or I should not be an applicant for this situation."

"Where is your father now?"

"He is in New York City."

"Possibly my husband knows him," added the lady. "Loring? Loring?" she continued, musing.

"I don't think he does," replied Bertha. "But, ma'am, my father does not know that I am trying to earn my own living and that of my sister. He has very recently failed in business. My friends don't know that I am an applicant for such a place; and, for reasons of my own, I wish to conceal my movements, at least for the present. You will excuse me from answering any questions in regard to my family."

Poor Bertha! It was her first attempt at deception of any kind, and she could hardly play the part she had chosen.

"I think I perfectly understand your position, and as Charley seems to like you so well, I shall engage you at the salary you named."

"Thank you, ma'am," exclaimed Bertha, astonished at the decision of Mrs. Byron. "You are very generous to take me without testimonials or reference; but I assure you your confidence shall not be undeserved."

"I am quite satisfied, or I shouldn't have ventured to engage you under these circumstances. Here, Charley, how would you like this young lady to take care of you?"

"Oh, ever so much, ma!" exclaimed Charley, jumping off his horse and seizing the new governess by the hand.

"She will teach you to read, Charley," added his mother.

"Oh, goody! I want to be able to read my picture books; but I can spell cat now; c-a-t, cat."

"Till you learn I will read them to you, Charley," said Bertha, who had already begun to feel a strong interest in her young charge.

"Have you any taste for music, Miss Loring?"

"I can play and sing a little," replied Bertha, modestly.

"Come and let me hear you play," said Charley, as he tugged away at the hand of Bertha, and finally dragged her into the parlor, where the piano was located.

"He is very fond of music," remarked Mrs. Byron, as she followed them into the parlor.

Bertha played several simple pieces for the amusement of the little boy, and played them so well that the mother was even more delighted than the child. Then, at the special request of Charley, she played and sang "Three Blind Mice," which suited him so well that he called for more. For an hour she engaged the attention of both her auditors; and then the heir of Blue Hill, as the estate of Mr. Byron was called, clamored for "pickers," which, rendered into the vernacular, meant pictures.

Charley produced pencils, paper and a slate, and insisted that Bertha should "make a house." She had early developed a decided taste and talent for drawing, and, up to the commencement of the summer vacation, she had taken lessons of an artist whose cottage was in the neighborhood of Woodville. Her teacher declared that she would make an artist, and quite a number of her pencil drawings adorned the walls of her father's house. In the extremity of her want and sorrow she had thought of applying her talent to a profitable use, and she had not yet given up the idea.

She took the pencil which Charley brought, and made a house which was entirely satisfactory. Then she made men, and horses, and carts, and other objects which the young gentleman called for, so that she soon became a prodigy in his eyes, and, of course, as the mother saw with the child's eyes, she was equally a wonder in her estimation.

When Charley began to grow weary of pictures, both of them were well rested from the fatigue of their walk, and the child proposed a ramble in the garden, where Bertha was just as pleasing and just as instructive as she had been at the piano and with the pencil.

At six o'clock Mr. Byron came home, and heard with astonishment the change which had been made in the domestic affairs of the family. Master Charley had considerable to say about his new governess, as his mother had already taught him to call her, and he recommended her so highly that the father was well satisfied with the change.

As soon as she had an opportunity she wrote to Ben, informing him what and where she was, and asking him to send her trunk to her. On the following day the trunk was brought down in the boat, and she had a visit from Ben and Noddy. The old man was glad to see her so well situated, but he had his doubts about the change of name. Noddy jumped and capered like an antelope, and astonished Charley by throwing back and forward somersets, and by such gyrations as the little fellow had never seen before. The visit was a pleasant one to all parties, and Ben and Noddy left with the promise to call again in a short time.

While Bertha was watching the boat as it sped on its way up the river, she heard a sharp cry from Charley, and on turning, saw him lying on the ground.

"Why, what's the matter, Charley?" she cried, lifting him up.

"I bumped my head and hurt me," replied he.

Bertha examined the injured member, and found a pretty smart bump on the summit of his cranium, which she washed in cold water from the river and rubbed it till Charley declared it was quite well.

"How did you do it?" asked she.

"I was trying to do what Noddy did, and hit my head upon a stone."

"You mustn't try to do such things as that."

"Noddy did it."

"Noddy is a little wild boy. I have told him a great many times not to do such things. It isn't pretty, and you must not try to do so again."

"I should like to do what Noddy did, and I mean to try it again."

"Don't, Charley; you may get a worse bump than you did this time."

"I don't care if I do; if Noddy did it, I can."

But before the forcible arguments which the governess brought forward Master Charley finally promised not to break his head in vain attempts to do what was neither pretty nor proper for the heir of Blue Hill to do.

A few days after the visit of the boatman she received a letter from Richard, which had been forwarded to her from Whitestone. He wrote in excellent spirits, and said he had obtained a situation on board of a gentleman's yacht, and was about to sail for Newport. He had seen his father in the Tombs. He was to be examined on the following day and fully expected to be discharged. This was all Richard said about his father. It was meager enough, and very unsatisfactory to Bertha. She had not the money to pay the expense of a visit to the city, or she would have asked leave of absence for a day to go and see him. She had written several letters to him, but had not yet received any reply, and therefore supposed they did not reach him.

Bertha soon found that her situation was not a bed of roses. Mrs. Byron was not an angel. Her temper was not angelic, and the governess was sometimes compelled to submit to harsh and unmerited rebuke, couched in such language as she had never heard before.

The hopeful heir of Blue Hill, though he could spell "cat" and knew who was President of the United States, was not yet fit to put on his wings and become a cherub. He had some of his mother's temper and a great deal of his own obstinacy. He was an only child, and as such had been indulged, as far as indulgence would go; and Bertha found that she was expected to lead, not to govern, him. If Charley wanted to jump into the river, she was to find arguments to convince him that the cold water was uncomfortable and might drown him. If he wanted to eat green apples, she was to persuade him not to do so, and not make him cry by taking them away from him.

One day he took a notion that certain unripe winter pears would be "good to take," and had actually bitten one of them, when Bertha, with as little force as was needful, took it from him and threw it away. Charley set up a howl which made the ground shake under him and brought his mother from the house. The heir of Blue Hill told his story, and Bertha was sharply scolded for crossing the dear little fellow.

When Mrs. Byron suggested that the young gentleman ought to commence learning his letters, the governess applied herself with becoming zeal to the task of teaching him those mysterious characters. For ten minutes Charley gave his attention; then he wanted her to read a story. In vain she coaxed him to learn the letters; it was plain that he had no taste for the heavy work of literature. Day after day she attempted to fasten his mind upon the A B C, but with no better success. She resorted to all the expedients she could devise, but Charley was as obstinate as a mule.

These were some of her trials—trials with Master Charley; trials with his mother. Bertha faithfully persevered and endured everything without a murmur. But her charge was sometimes a little lamb, as pretty and as cunning as child could be; and there were hours of sunshine—oases in the desert of trial and care.

When Bertha had been at Blue Hill about a week Mr. Byron gave a large dinner party, and the house was filled with all fine folks of the surrounding country. Mrs. Byron was very much afraid Charley would get into his "tantrums" in the presence of the company, and thus convince them that he was not an angel, in spite of his velvet tunic and his lace-frilled trousers. During the dinner hour, therefore—a period in which Charley was peculiarly liable to be attacked by unaccountable humors—Bertha was required to keep him in the nursery, and also to keep him in excellent temper.

By dint of extraordinary tact and perseverance she succeeded in accomplishing both these ends, and congratulated herself upon the hope that she should thus escape the unwelcome infliction of seeing any of the visitors. It was quite probable that among them were many friends of her father, and the fear of being recognized, and her little deception exposed, was terrible. The dinner hour was a fashionable one, and before the party rose from the table Charley's bedtime had arrived, and she was on the point of disposing of him for the night, when Mrs. Byron entered the nursery.

"The company have just gone to the parlor, and they all insist upon seeing Charley," said she.

Bertha was appalled; but it was useless to offer any objections, and she proceeded to prepare her charge for the ordeal.

"I suppose it is not necessary for me to appear with him," said she, in an indifferent tone, which but ill concealed her anxiety.

"Certainly it is," replied Mrs. Byron, sharply. "You must go with him, and be sure that you make him appear to the best advantage. You can tell him some cunning little things to say before he goes down. Let him come into the room with his hat on and his little cane in his hand."

"Wouldn't you excuse me from going with him?" pleaded Bertha.

"Certainly not."

"I will go with him to the door and tell him what to say," added Bertha.

"I thought you were brought up in a good family," sneered Mrs. Byron. "You surely are not afraid to appear in company."

"Not afraid to, ma'am, but I do not like to do so."

"Whether you like it or not, you must do so. Now be sure that Charley appears well and shows himself to the best advantage," said Mrs. Byron, as she sailed out of the room.

There was no alternative, and Bertha prepared for the trial. Charley's plumed hat was put upon his head, his cane placed in his hand and he was duly marched into the presence of the company.

CHAPTER 13

BERTHA LOSES HER SITUATION

Master Charley strutted into the parlor, cane in hand, and was warmly greeted by the guests, who, as a matter of politeness, if nothing else, were in duty bound to admire his curly head and his cunning manners. For a time, therefore, Bertha escaped observation, and the heir of Blue Hill was the center of attraction.

"I can spell cat; c-a-t, cat," roared Charley; "and I can spell dog; d-o-g, dog."

"Now, who is governor of New York, Charley?" whispered Bertha.

"Oh, I know!" and Charley scratched his head and disarranged the curls, to the horror of his mother. "Oh, I know who is governor of New York; it is Capt. Kidd; and he buried lots of money round here, somewhere."

The company laughed heartily at this sally, and thought it was very cunning; but Bertha blushed at the carelessness of her pupil, and Mrs. Byron looked daggers at the governess. The exhibition of Charley's quick points promised to be a failure; and Bertha was sadly perplexed, for she felt that she was not giving satisfaction.

But there was still one more hope left. She had taught Charley to play "Days of Absence" with one finger on the piano, and she thought he might possibly make a sensation with this, if he had not forgotten it, as he had almost everything else. She placed him upon the stool, and, putting the finger in the right place, the young gentleman went through this performance in a very creditable manner, very much to the surprise even of his mother, who had not heard him do it. The guests clapped their hands, and expressed their admiration in no measured terms, which so excited the vanity of the child that he immediately proceeded to perform another astounding feat, which was not put down in the program. This was no less than throwing a back somerset, in imitation of Noddy Newman.

If the experiment had not been a failure, no doubt it would have been received with rapturous applause, as everything he did was received; but Charley was not quite equal to a back somerset, and struck the floor upon the top of his head. The new sensation was decidedly unpleasant to the heir of Blue Hill, and was not at all agreeable to the company. It was followed by a yell that would have been creditable to a tiger in the jungle of Hindustan. Bertha ran to his assistance, picked him up, and rubbed the bump which had been so suddenly developed. It was the bump of self-esteem naturally enlarged, which was entirely unnecessary, for Charley had a superabundance before the accident.

The sympathizing guests gathered around the wounded hero, and endeavored to console him; but he bawled incessantly, and refused to be comforted. Mrs. Byron was shocked, and declared that the mishap had resulted from the careless governess introducing the boy to bad company. But whatever the cause, and whatever the efforts used to induce Master Charley to moderate his excessive grief, he wept and roared as one without hope.

"Take him to the nursery," said Mrs. Byron, in a whisper to Bertha.

"Come upstairs with me, Charley, and I will make a house for you," said Bertha.

"I won't go upstairs. I don't want any of your old pictures," bawled the discomfited hero.

"Come up with me, and I will sing 'Three Blind Mice' to you."

"I won't."

"We will play horse, then."

"I don't want to play horse. I am going to stay here as long as I please."

Bertha was tempted to pick him up, and carry him out of the room; but this would be violation of all rule and precedent. In vain she coaxed him; in vain she promised to play everything and sing everything. Charley had lost his temper, and nothing could move him. A spoiled child on exhibition, especially when he performs after the manner of Master Charley on the present occasion, is disgusting to all except his parents. Mrs. Byron was not satisfied with the conduct of her hopeful; but instead of regarding it as the result of a want of discipline, she attributed it all to the mismanagement of the governess.

Bertha would have brought the scene to a conclusion, however unpleasant, without delay, if she had dared to do so; but as Master Charley must have his own way, no matter who suffered, or what consequences followed, he was not taken from the room by the strong hand of authority. He bawled till his throat must have been sorer than his head, and the company were tired of the music.

At last, a gentleman, despairing of any relief, took out his watch, and offered to show the works to the disconsolate heir. This was a rare treat, and Charley had the grace to yield the point, and submit to a treaty of peace, or at least to a suspension of hostilities.

"How do you do, Miss Grant?" said a gentleman who had been observing Bertha with close attention for some time, as he stepped forward and extended his hand.

She took it, blushed deeply, and stammered out a reply, for Mrs. Byron was standing by her side.

"How is your father?" asked the gentleman.

"He is not very well. I have not seen him lately."

"I have frequently met you at Woodville; perhaps you do not remember me."

"Yes, sir, I do."

"I have been at the South for some months, and returned yesterday. Do you still reside at Woodville?"

"No, sir."

"You are visiting your friends here, I suppose. It is very kind of you to attempt to manage that child," he added, in a low tone, as Mrs. Byron's attention was called to a rupture between Charley and his new friend, whose watch the dear little fellow insisted upon picking to pieces.

"He is very hard to manage," replied Bertha.

"A spoiled child," added the gentleman, as Mrs. Byron returned to the spot.

"My governess is wholly incompetent," said she, angrily, for she had heard the last remark. "Charley is a good boy, and, when properly managed, is as gentle as a lamb, Mr. Gray."

"He appears to be," added the gentleman, satirically. "He evidently has a sweet temper, and in due time will make a great and good man."

Mrs. Byron did not understand these remarks, but took them as a compliment, and her anger was partially appeased.

"He has had enough to try the temper of a saint. He nearly died with cholera three days ago from eating green apples, of which the governess permitted him to partake."

Mr. Gray looked at Bertha, and evidently did not believe this statement, for the sudden coloring of Bertha's cheek seemed to refute the falsehood.

"Do I understand you that Miss Grant is the child's governess?"

"Miss Loring," added Mrs. Byron.

"But this is the daughter of Mr. Grant, of Woodville," said the gentleman, who was perplexed by the name and the relation which she bore to the family.

"My father has met with some heavy reverses," stammered Bertha. "I am engaged as a governess here."

"Pardon me," said Mr. Gray, who was now greatly embarrassed. "As I said, I have recently come home, after an absence of some months, and had not heard of the unpleasant position of your father's affairs."

"Miss Grant?" said the lady of the house. "Miss Loring, you can retire," she added, in a loud tone.

Bertha was too glad to obey this haughty command to object even to the tone in which it was uttered. But when she had gone, Mrs. Byron heard more about Mr. Grant and his affairs; for there were several present who were acquainted with him, and all had read the history of his alleged fall in the papers. She learned that the father of her governess was even then a prisoner in the Tombs.

"To think that I have placed my only child in the care of such a person!" exclaimed Mrs. Byron.

"Miss Bertha Grant is a very excellent young lady," Mr. Gray ventured to suggest.

"She is an impostor!" said Mrs. Byron, who seemed to feel that the governess was the cause of all her mortal trials.

"At Woodville she was regarded as a young lady of splendid abilities, and her mission to the poor children of Dunk's Hollow was the admiration of all the neighborhood," added Mr. Gray. "I know of no person to whom I would more willingly intrust my children."

"She is an impostor!" persisted Mrs. Byron. "That is enough to condemn her;" and leaving Charley to entertain the company in his fascinating way, she flounced out of the room, and hastened to the nursery, to which Bertha had already retreated.

"Miss Loring, you have deceived and disappointed me," she began, still flushed with anger.

"I am sorry I deceived you, Mrs. Byron, and I hope you will forgive me, for I meant no harm to you."

"You are an impostor!"

"No, ma'am, I am not. I am just what I represented myself to be."

"Your father is in prison for fraud."

"That is his misfortune, but it is not my fault," replied Bertha, indignant at this brutal treatment.

"Misfortune? Yes, that is what they always call it when a man commits a crime."

"My father has committed no crime."

"You came here under a false name. You have imposed upon me. I don't know what you are, even now. At any rate, you are not a fit person to watch over the innocent life of my only child. I tremble for him even now, after you have been here only a week. Of course you understand me."

"Your words are plain enough."

"I don't want you to remain here another night," added the angry woman. "I have trusted you too long."

"I hope I have not abused your confidence," said Bertha, overwhelmed by this outburst of abuse.

"I have not counted my spoons since you came."

"Madam, that is an insult that no lady would put upon an unprotected girl. I will leave your house immediately," answered Bertha, almost stunned by this unfeeling charge.

"As quick as possible, if you please," sneered the lady. "I dare not lose sight of you."

Bertha stepped into the adjoining room, and in a few moments was dressed ready to leave the house.

"I should like to look into your trunk before you go," said Mrs. Byron, whose malice seemed to be unlimited.

"You cannot, madam," replied Bertha, firmly, but respectfully.

"But I think I shall. Since I have found out what you are, I have a great many doubts. Give me the key of your trunk."

"No, madam, I will not. I will submit to no further insult."

"I will see if you won't."

"If you proceed any further, madam, I will appeal to Mr. Gray for protection. He was my father's friend, and I hope he is mine. I will leave your house at once, and send for my trunk as soon as I can."

"Not till your trunk has been examined."

"Very well, madam; I will appeal to Mr. Gray," and she passed out of the room.

"Stop, Miss Loring."

Bertha paused in the hall.

"If there is nothing in your trunk but what belongs to you, you need not fear to have it examined."

"There is nothing but my property in it; but I will not submit to such an insult."

"You can go! and if Mr. Byron thinks it necessary to search the trunk, he will do so."

"You have forgotten to pay me my salary, madam," said Bertha.

"Dare you ask for payment after what has happened?"

"I think I am justly entitled to what I have earned."

"I don't think so, and you can go."

"But I want my wages, madam."

"I do not owe you anything. You imposed upon me, and you have done Charley more harm than good. He never behaved as he did this evening before since he was born."

"I think I have done my duty faithfully; at least I have tried to do it. I have not money enough to pay my fare to the city, and I hope you will not keep back my wages."

"I shall pay you nothing."

"I shall be very sorry to appeal to Mr. Gray for assistance, but I shall have to ask him to lend me a few dollars."

"You impudent hussy!" exclaimed Mrs. Byron, in a great rage, as she again found herself in a difficult position.

Mr. Gray was a wealthy and influential person, and she would have given any sum rather than permit him to know anything about the matter. Bertha said no more, but walked down the stairs, intending to call Mr. Gray from the parlor, and tell him the whole truth. When she reached the lower hall, she heard the screams of Master Charley, who had evidently had a falling out with the owner of the watch.

"I want Miss Loring!" screamed the little ruffian.

She was about to approach the open door of the parlor, when Mrs. Bryon rushed down the stairs, and in more gentle tones than she had heard her use since the first day she came into the house, called her by name. She paused, and the lady joined her.

"Here is three dollars. I believe that is what I owe you—is it not?"

"Yes, madam; thank you."

"Peter has a horse and wagon at the door, and he will carry your trunk for you."

"Thank you, ma'am; you are very kind," said Bertha, surprised at the sudden change in the manner of the lady.

The powerful name of Mr. Gray had wrought the change, with, perhaps, a consciousness that she had exceeded the bounds of humanity and decency.

The lady stepped into the parlor and closed the door behind her, that no one might witness the departure of the discharged governess. Bertha found in Peter a ready friend, and in a few moments she was seated in the wagon by his side, with her trunk in front of her.

"Where shall I drive you, Miss Loring?" asked Peter, as they proceeded down the hill to the road.

"I hardly know, Peter," replied Bertha, sadly. "I have no place to go."

"No place to go!" exclaimed he. "What are you leaving at this hour of night for, then?"

"I was obliged to leave."

"Ah! I see how it is. I was afraid that brat would be the death of you; and when I heard him screeching in the parlor, I thought there would be a row for somebody. Then you have been discharged?"

"I have."

"Turned out of the house at this hour of night, with no place to go! That woman has no more soul than a brickbat."

"Is there a hotel in the village, Peter?"

"There is; but it is no place for a girl like you. If you will go to my cottage, you shall have a poor man's welcome."

"Thank you, Peter. I shall be very grateful to you if you will let me remain with you till morning."

"I will, with all my heart."

Peter was head groom at Blue Hill, and his house was only a short distance from the residence of Mr. Byron. Peter's wife received her kindly and conducted her to the little spare chamber which was appropriated to her use.

The groom evidently understood the temper of the mistress of Blue Hill well enough to comprehend the nature of the difficulty which had driven Bertha from her place, and neither he nor his wife asked any questions. Although it was quite early in the evening, the poor girl preferred to retire, and her hostess offered no objection.

The events of the evening had been so rapid and unexpected that Bertha was entirely unprepared for the shock which had so suddenly fallen upon her. Again she was alone and friendless in the world, and she could hardly expect another lucky incident would supply her with a home, as had been the case only a week before. But she was a little better off than she had been then, for she had three dollars in her purse, with which to pay her fare to the city.

Before she went to sleep she committed herself to the care of her heavenly Father, and felt confident that He would guide her steps, and protect her in the midst of the trials which were before her.

At breakfast the next morning, when Bertha announced her purpose of going to the city, Peter offered to drive her down to the ferry, where she could cross the river, and take the train on the other side. She accepted his offer, and as soon as he could get the horse, he returned from the stable.

In a short time Bertha was embarked on the ferry, with many thanks to Peter and his wife for their kindness, which, she assured him, should never be forgotten. A ride of less than an hour brought her to the great city, where everybody seemed to be rushing to and fro, as though the salvation of the world depended upon the rapidity of their movements. None of them took any notice of poor Bertha, and she was more alone in the midst of the multitude than she had been amid the rural scenes she had just left.

She knew not what to do, or where to go, and having left her trunk in charge of the baggage master at the railroad station, she wandered down Broadway.

CHAPTER 14

BERTHA VISITS HER FATHER'S OFFICE

Bertha knew enough of the perils of the city to make her tremble, when she considered that she was alone and unprotected. The prospect of finding suitable employment was exceedingly hopeless. Though she had often been in the city, and knew the principal localities, everything seemed strange to her; the houses and the streets wore a different aspect, for she was not now the daughter of the rich broker, but the child of want, seeking the opportunity to fulfill what had become the great mission of her existence.

Though her first object was to obtain a situation where she might procure the means of subsistence, this was not the mission of Bertha Grant. She had in her mind, clearly and hopefully defined, a higher and holier purpose. As at Woodville, in the midst of luxury and plenty, she did not live only to enjoy them; she now felt that she had been sent into the world with a great work given her to perform. An earnest and true man, from his pulpit in Whitestone, had given her the idea, and she had pondered and cherished it till it became a principle.

She believed she had been created to do good to her fellow beings, and with this noble thought in her heart she had gone upon her mission to the poor children of Dunk's Hollow. He who spoke in Whitestone the words and the spirit of Him of Nazareth spoke through Bertha to the friendless and despised little ones who gathered around her at the Glen. His words and her words, spoken in faith and hope, and embodied in good and generous deeds, were to yield their hundredfold; and though Bertha had been withdrawn from her labors, the seeds which she had sown were still growing. Though some might perish, others would live, and thrive and mature.

In the same faith and hope which had led her to gather together the children of Dunk's Hollow, she was now laboring to save her father and her brother—her father from suffering and sorrow, her brother from himself. This was the present mission of Bertha Grant; and it was a part of the great purpose of her existence. While she was in want she could do nothing. The body must be fed and clothed, and if she could obtain employment that would relieve her from absolute want, she would be in condition to prosecute the greater work of the hour.

Full of these thoughts she walked down Broadway, with nothing to encourage her, and without any plan or expectation to guide her doubtful footsteps. Slowly she threaded her way through the dense crowd that always throngs the street, till she came to City Hall Park. All the way she had looked in vain for any suggestion that might aid her in accomplishing her purpose. In a few hours more the night would come. She dared not go to a hotel in the great city, and she trembled to think of being friendless and homeless in those streets where villains choose darkness for deeds of sin and violence.

The thought filled her with terror, but it inspired her with new resolution. There was something to be done, and the time for doing it was short. Yet where should she go? She could not answer this question, and involuntarily she continued her walk down Broadway, till she came to Wall Street. She was now near her father's office, and she determined to go and look at it, if nothing more.

It was a familiar locality, for she had often been to see her father during business hours. To her astonishment she found the office open, and her father's clerk in his usual place at the desk. This looked hopeful to her, and she entered, with a beating heart, to inquire about her father.

"Miss Grant!" exclaimed the clerk, as she came in.

"Can you tell me anything about my father?" asked Bertha, as she seated herself in the chair which the clerk offered her.

"I am sorry to say that I cannot give you any good news from him," replied Mr. Sherwood, gloomily.

"Where is he now?"

"He is where he was," said the clerk, embarrassed.

"In the prison, you mean."

"Yes, in the Tombs; but I am certain that he will come out without the stain of dishonor upon him."

"I feel, I know, that he has been guilty of no crime," added Bertha, earnestly.

"I suppose you understand the circumstances under which he was arrested?"

"I do not."

"It is a rather complicated affair. He was arrested on the charge of fraud."

"So I have understood."

"But he is no more guilty of fraud than I am; and if we can only get a chance to let the truth out, we shall make the matter plain to the whole world. Grayle is at the bottom of the whole affair; he is your father's enemy."

"He is a very rude and hard man," said Bertha, recalling the incidents of her departure from Woodville.

"Three or four years ago your father spoiled a dishonest speculation in which Grayle and others were engaged; this made him an enemy, though they still kept on good terms together. Some months since Mr. Grant borrowed fifty thousand dollars of him, giving him certain English securities as collateral."

"I really don't know what you mean," said Bertha.

"The securities were certain papers, by which Brace Brothers, an English banking firm, supposed to be very wealthy, promised to pay certain sums of money," continued the clerk, smiling at the perplexed look of Bertha. "In other words, Brace Brothers promised to pay your father—or the holder of the papers—twelve thousand pounds."

"I understand that."

"This money was to be drawn in bills of exchange, or orders. Now, when your father wanted a large sum for immediate use, he gave them to Mr. Grayle as security, because the bills of exchange were not to be drawn till September. The very next steamer that came in brought intelligence of the suspension of Brace Brothers—that is, they had stopped payment—did not pay their notes and other obligations."

"I understand it very well."

"Well, Grayle declared that your father knew these securities were worthless when he gave them to him, and immediately accused him of fraud. He came into the office very much excited, and talked to your father as no gentleman ever talked to another. Your father resented the charge, which made Grayle all the more angry."

"But how could he accuse my father of fraud, when all this happened before it was known that Brace Brothers had suspended?"

"There was some reason," said the clerk, after a pause. "One of Grayle's friends had a letter, which had come before the transaction, in which Brace Brothers mentioned their financial embarrassments; but I am certain your father had no suspicion that they were weak. In fact," said Mr. Sherwood, in a very low tone, "I have a letter, which I carry in my pocket since your father was arrested, that will set the matter all right. A friend of mine gave it to me. Grayle would give a thousand dollars for this letter," added the clerk, with a triumphant air.

"I hope you will save him," replied Bertha.

"I know I shall. Our own correspondence with Brace Brothers shows that they believed themselves to be sound. But this letter will save him, if nothing else will. All we want is to get the matter before the court. Grayle keeps getting it put off, for if the truth comes out it will ruin him."

"He has secured Woodville," added Bertha.

"That was the only weak thing your father did. Grayle went so far that your father was alarmed, and attempted to save his honor at the expense of his property. He gave Grayle a bill of sale of Woodville and all it contained, to keep him quiet for a few days, till he could raise the money to pay him. The villain then arrested your father and took possession of Woodville."

"The paper said my father was going to leave the country."

"All nonsense! He had no more idea of leaving the country than I had. Grayle watched him all the time; and when he went over to the British steamer to see a friend, who was going to Europe, he had him arrested, and then circulated the story which you read in the newspaper. Everybody believes just now that Mr. Grant is a common swindler; but we will set that matter right before long."

"I am sure I hope so. Could I see my father?"

"I am afraid not. Your brother got in, and saw him; but since then orders have been given to admit no one but his counsel. They wouldn't let me in. Grayle is playing a deep game, and has probably used his influence to prevent your father from seeing his friends. He is a villain."

Mr. Sherwood's opinions were decided, and were very emphatically delivered. They were full of hope and encouragement to Bertha, and she rejoiced that she had been led to visit the office. But, although she was comforted and assured by the intelligence she had gained, there was nothing in it which promised to supply her immediate wants. She was still homeless and friendless, for she had not the courage to place herself under the protection of Mr. Sherwood. He was a young man, and had been with her father but a few months. She was not prepared to adopt this course until all other resources had failed.

There was nothing in the facts she had just learned to change her purpose. Her father might get out of prison, but he was a ruined man. Mr. Sherwood might be mistaken in his estimate of the value of the letter in his possession. The duty of providing for herself and Fanny seemed to be just as imperative as ever.

Though she was not yet willing to ask the protection of her father's clerk, the time might come within a few hours when she might be glad to do so. He was ignorant of her real situation, and supposed she was comfortably located in the house of some friend or relative.

"Where shall I find you, Mr. Sherwood, in case I should wish to see you again?" asked Bertha.

"You will find me here at all hours of the day and night. I have not been out of the office for more than half an hour at once since your father was arrested. I sleep on that sofa. Grayle is an unscrupulous wretch, and I don't think he would hesitate to take any papers in the office which would serve his purpose; or even to break in, if he has the courage to do so."

"What a terrible man he must be!" added Bertha.

"He offered me a situation in his office the day after your father was arrested. I think he would be willing to buy me up at any price."

"I am sure my father will be grateful to you."

"Your father always used me well, and I will not desert him if all the rest of the world does."

"I am very thankful that he has so good a friend."

"Oh, I only wish to do as I would be done by. If you should want anything, Miss Grant, you can call upon me. There was a small sum of money in the office when your father was arrested, though I suppose it will all come in use to pay the lawyers, and other expenses."

"Thank you; I don't need anything at present," replied Bertha, who would not have touched a dollar that could be serviceable in effecting her father's release.

At this point an elderly gentleman entered the office, and began to make inquiries of Mr. Sherwood concerning her father. He looked at Bertha for a moment, and appeared to be excited. She thought his countenance seemed familiar to her, though she was confident she had never seen him before. The clerk, perhaps thinking it would not be pleasant for her to hear her father's situation discussed by a stranger, conducted her into the private office, and gave her the morning paper—the *Herald*.

Bertha wondered who the gentleman was, as she glanced over the columns of the paper. His face was strangely familiar, yet she was positive she had never seen him. But her attention was soon withdrawn from him by an advertisement in the paper, which caught her eye. An old gentleman, an invalid, advertised for a well-educated young lady, to read to him, and act as amanuensis.

"If I could only get that place!" said she to herself, as she wrote down on a slip of paper the address mentioned in the advertisement.

There would be hundreds of applicants for the situation; but she could try to obtain it, and she resolved to do so without a moment's delay. As she passed through the other office, where the stranger was engaged in earnest conversation with the clerk, she said that she would call again some other time, and hastened down the stairs to the street.

The house of the invalid gentleman was in the upper part of the city, and she took the street car uptown, lest some other applicant should obtain the place before her. Without much difficulty she found the house. It was an elegant establishment, and on the door was the name of "F. Presby." With a trembling hand, she rang the bell, which was answered by a man in a white jacket.

"I wish to see Mr. Presby," replied Bertha.

"Which Mr. Presby?"

"The old gentleman—the invalid."

"Another person to answer the advertisement," said a female voice in the entry, beyond the inner door. "Tell her he is not at home, John."

"Not at home, miss," repeated the man in the white jacket.

"When will he be at home?" asked Bertha.

"He has left town, and will not be back until next week."

"But he advertised for a young lady."

"Yes, miss, he did; but, you see, the old gentleman is crazy, and don't know what he wants. At any rate, he don't want any young lady."

Poor Bertha's heart sank within her, as the nice place which she had hoped to obtain proved to be a mere shadow, and she stood gazing at the servant with a look of despair.

"Not at home, miss," repeated the man, partially closing the door, as a hint for her to leave.

She turned and descended the steps, the man closing the door with a slam. But she had scarcely reached the sidewalk, before she heard the door open again. She turned to discover the cause, and saw a tall, pale old gentleman, with a dressing gown on, standing at the door.

"Do you wish to see me?" asked he, in feeble tones.

"I called to see Mr. Presby," replied Bertha, a ray of hope again lighting up her soul.

"Come in, if you please."

But the servant had told her that old Mr. Presby was crazy, and did not want a young lady to read to him. The thought of throwing herself into the company of a lunatic was not pleasing; but the sad, pale old gentleman looked so mild and inoffensive that she concluded there must be some mistake, and she followed him into the house.

CHAPTER 15

BERTHA MYSTIFIED BY STRANGE THINGS

The old gentleman conducted Bertha up the stairs to the large front room which was fitted up as a library. It was furnished in a plain, old-fashioned manner, and was well supplied with sofas, lounges and easy-chairs. As they entered this room, the old gentleman closed the door behind them, and offered her a chair.

Bertha almost wished she had not come in, when Mr. Presby closed the door, for being alone with an insane man was the most terrible thing she could imagine. She did not at first dare to take the chair to which the old gentleman beckoned her, but lingered near the door, ready to make her escape when she should discover the first symptom of insanity in the invalid.

"Be seated, if you please," said the old gentleman.

"Thank you, sir," stammered Bertha, keeping near the door, and gazing at the invalid with the deepest anxiety.

But then it occurred to her that the rude servant had told her Mr. Presby was out of town, which was certainly a falsehood; and perhaps the statement that he was crazy was equally false. She had never seen an insane person; but Mr. Presby did not look any different from any other person. He was sad and pale, and seemed to be harmless.

"Won't you take a seat?" asked he again, in a tone so mild that she was almost convinced he was not crazy.

She had heard that insane people are sometimes quite rational, and only have fits of madness at times. This might be the case with Mr. Presby, and he might, at any moment, become a raving maniac. But she took the chair, though she trembled as she did so, and kept one eye upon the door all the time.

"You wished to see me," continued the old gentleman, as he seated himself near her—much nearer than she wished to have him under the circumstances.

"Yes, sir," replied Bertha, looking him in the eye, that she might discover the first symptom of wildness in season to make her escape before he could proceed to violence.

"Don't be alarmed," added Mr. Presby, with a smile, as he evidently noticed her agitation.

"I—I'm—not alarmed," stammered Bertha, in doubt whether she should apply for the situation.

"You are, I presume, an applicant for the place which I advertised in the morning paper."

"Yes, sir; I called to see about that; but—I—I don't know as the place will suit me," answered she, still very much embarrassed at the thought of becoming reader and amanuensis for a crazy man.

"Well, my child, I don't wish you to take the situation if you think it will not suit you," added Mr. Presby, with a fatherly smile. "What is your name?"

"Bertha Grant, sir."

"Why do you think the place would not suit you?"

"Because—I, really, sir—"

"You seem to have changed your mind very suddenly."

"The servant told me you were out of town—"

"And out of my head," said the invalid, with a smile. "I begin to understand why you think the situation will not suit you. The servant told you that Mr. Presby was crazy, and did not want any young lady."

"Yes, sir," replied Bertha, frankly.

"I am not crazy. I thank God that amid the misfortunes He has visited upon me, I am still permitted to enjoy my reason unimpaired. No, child, I am not insane."

"I am so glad to hear it!" exclaimed Bertha.

But the glowing expression with which she received this assurance quickly gave place to a sad look again, as she considered that the invalid might not be aware of his own infirmity.

"You have some doubts," added he, as he observed the change upon her face. "It is sad for me to have to defend myself from such a charge. You know that John told you one falsehood."

"Yes, sir; and I am satisfied," replied Bertha; "but it seems very strange to me."

"If you would like the situation, I think I can convince you that I am not crazy."

"I would like it very much, sir, if you would please to give me the place."

"Perhaps you will not suit me," added Mr. Presby.

"I will try to do so, sir."

"You are very young."

"I shall be fourteen in a short time."

"Younger than I thought you were; it will be hard for a girl like you to be shut up with an old man like me."

"I shall not mind that, sir."

"And there will be a great many annoyances and trials to endure."

"I will try to be faithful and patient."

"I suppose there have been a dozen applicants at the door for the place this forenoon, but you are the first that I have seen. They were all sent away, as you were. I should not have seen you if I had not happened to overhear the conversation between you and John in the hall."

"How very strange!" said Bertha, not able to comprehend this singular state of things.

"You will understand it soon enough. I like your appearance, young as you are; and as I may not see another applicant, I am the more desirous of engaging you, if you will answer my purpose. I presume you have been well educated, or you would not have applied for the place."

Bertha briefly stated the history of her education, which seemed to be satisfactory to Mr. Presby. He then questioned her in regard to her family, and, without telling any more than was necessary, she informed him in regard to her past life. He was not inquisitive, and she passed the examination without informing him what her father's first name was, or where he had resided.

"Now, Miss Grant, I should like to hear you read."

He then handed her Kirk White's poems, and she read a couple of pages.

"You read very well indeed for one so young, and you appear to understand what you read. Now I will dictate a letter for you to write, and if your penmanship is plain and distinct, you will satisfy me in every respect."

Mr. Presby dictated to Bertha a letter of about a page in length. Her taste and skill in drawing had materially improved her writing, and she wrote a beautiful hand, much larger and plainer than fashionably educated young ladies usually write.

"That is admirable!" exclaimed Mr. Presby, as she handed him the sheet. "It is as plain as print. I commend your hand to the bookkeepers downtown. I can read that writing."

"I am very glad it suits you, sir," said Bertha, delighted with the success of her examination.

"You have spelled all the words right, and the letter is neat and well arranged. I suppose you know something about arithmetic and geography?"

"Yes, sir; I am very willing to be examined."

"No, I will not trouble you any further. If the place will suit you, it is yours."

"Thank you, sir."

Bertha was sure it would suit her, if Mr. Presby was not insane; and she was well satisfied now that he was not.

"You have not spoken of the salary, sir," suggested Bertha, who had some doubts on this subject.

"You may suit yourself about that, Miss Grant," replied Mr. Presby, with a smile. "Money is the least of my cares in this world."

"If you thought four dollars a week was not too much," said she, after some hesitation.

"I will give you five with pleasure," added Mr. Presby. "It is of no consequence what I pay, if you answer my purpose."

"You are very kind and very generous, sir; and I will do the best I can to please you."

"That is all I require; and you need not come in the morning till ten o'clock."

Ten o'clock! Then she had no home, after all, and she must find a place to board somewhere in the vicinity. The five dollars a week seemed to melt away all at once, for it would take three dollars a week to pay her board, and there was only two left to pay Fanny's board, and nothing for clothes and other expenses.

"Where do you live?" asked Mr. Presby. "I suppose you will want to go home before it is very dark at night."

"I have no home," answered Bertha, sadly.

"No home! Poor child! Then your parents are dead?"

She did not dare to tell him that her father was in prison; so she made no reply.

"But you shall have a home here," continued Mr. Presby, rising and opening a door which led into a small chamber over the front hall. "You shall have this room, and take your meals with me."

"Thank you, sir; I shall never be able to repay you for your kindness."

"Poor child! This is the happiest day I have known for a long time. I thank the Lord for sending you to me, for we shall be a blessing to each other."

Bertha could not help crying, the old gentleman was so kind. She was sure now that he could not be crazy; and she wondered more than ever at the strange conduct of John, and the female voice she had heard in the hall.

She looked into the chamber, and found it was nicely furnished, and had a very pleasant aspect. With the devout old gentleman she thanked God for conducting her to this new home. She felt Mr. Presby would not turn her out of the house, even if he should find out that her father was a prisoner in the Tombs.

"Poor child," said Mr. Presby, which seemed to be growing into a favorite expression with him. "You said your name was—"

"Bertha Grant, sir."

"Bertha; I shall call you Bertha, for you are only a child now, and I mean to be a father to you, if you are a good girl, as I am sure you will be. Poor child! no home, and no friends."

The old man walked slowly up and down the room, as he uttered these words, and seemed to be thinking of something.

"I wish I had a better home than this for you, poor child," said Mr. Presby, stopping in front of her chair.

"I could not ask a better home," replied Bertha.

"Poor child! It is hearts that make home, not fine rooms, rich carpets, and costly furniture," added Mr. Presby, with a deep sigh, as he shook his head, and resumed his walk. "Hearts, not rooms and furniture," he murmured several times.

"I could ask no kinder heart than yours to warm my home," said Bertha, pitying the old man, he was so sad.

"Poor child! I love you already," exclaimed Mr. Presby, as he paused by her side, bent over and kissed her on the forehead, while a great tear dropped from his sunken eye upon her brow.

Bertha thought the old gentleman acted very strangely. There was a mystery connected with him which she could not penetrate. The conduct of John, and the female who had spoken, added to the mystery, rather than assisted in its solution. It was evident that they had prevented several applicants for the situation she had obtained from seeing the invalid, and had attempted to prevent her from doing so. Why they should act in this manner was unaccountable to her; but she had no desire to pry into matters which did not concern her.

"This shall be your home, my child," said Mr. Presby, pausing again, and looking tenderly upon her.

"Thank you, sir. You fixed my wages before you knew that I had no other home. You will wish to change the sum now."

"No, child, no!" answered Mr. Presby, impatiently. "Now, do not say anything more about money. It has been the bane of my life. I do not like the sound of the word. You shall have five dollars a week, or ten, or any other sum you desire, only let me have one true friend in the world, and I care not for all the gold in the universe."

"Pardon me, sir," said Bertha, deeply moved by the earnestness of the old gentleman; for, as he spoke, the tears coursed down his pale, wrinkled cheek, and his soul seemed to be filled with anguish. "I would not have mentioned the subject again, if it had not been a matter of great consequence to me. I have a sister in the country, and I only wish to earn money enough to support her."

"I knew that one so young could not love money. It has been a curse to me. God has punished me by making me rich. I am worth at least half a million of dollars. I own houses and lands, stocks, bonds and mortgages, I have the notes of rich men in my safe, and I have over a hundred thousand dollars in the banks; but I would give all I have in the world, every dollar, for a poor cottage in the country, if I could have with it the respect and affection of my—of my—of those whom Heaven sent to bless my declining years, and smooth my pathway to the grave."

The old man dropped into his chair, and wept as though his heart would break. Bertha tried to comfort him. She brushed back the long, white locks from his forehead, and kissed his wrinkled brow. Gentle-hearted as she was, she could not help weeping with him.

"Poor child!" sobbed Mr. Presby. "You must not love me; if you do, others will hate you."

"I wish I could do something to make you happy," replied Bertha.

"No; they will hate you, if you do."

"Who will hate me?"

The old man looked at her in silence for a moment.

"I dare not tell you," said he. "I am a great sufferer. God has sorely afflicted me; but I try to be patient and resigned to my lot. It is hard, very hard."

Mr. Presby wiped his eyes, and, after a struggle, calmed his strong emotion.

"Come, Bertha, you shall read to me now," he added.

"What shall I read?" asked she.

"You shall select something yourself."

She took the Bible, and read the twenty-third Psalm, and then a portion of the Sermon on the Mount.

CHAPTER 16

THE STORY OF A FAMILY QUARREL

Mr. Presby was comforted by the passages which Bertha read, and perhaps the sympathy she extended to the suffering invalid was hardly less soothing than the words of the Scripture. Though she had gathered some idea of the nature of her patron's troubles from the conversation she had had with him, yet she was still ignorant of his relations with the other occupants of the house. She comprehended that his children were unkind and ungrateful to him, and this seemed so unnatural and terrible to her that she pitied the old gentleman from the depths of her soul.

After she had finished reading the Bible, Mr. Presby remained silent and thoughtful for a long time. He seemed to be meditating upon the passages read, and she did not disturb him; but she could not help calling to mind the statement of John that he was insane. His conduct was certainly very singular; but if his children, those who should have loved him, who should have comforted him and humored his weakness—if they had turned against him, it would be quite enough to explain even more strange behavior than he had yet exhibited.

He rose from his easy-chair, and paced the room, as he had done before; but he was calm, and appeared to be more resigned. He did not talk to himself, as he had done; and whether he was insane or not, Bertha had ceased to be afraid of him, and even felt some confidence that she could manage him if he should have a paroxysm.

"Poor child!" said he, at last, as he paused in his walk. "I am old and thoughtless; you have no home, and I suppose you have no clothing. Come, we will go out and buy some for you."

"I have plenty of clothing, sir. My trunk is at the railroad station," replied Bertha.

"We will go out and get it, then. The carriage comes to take me out to ride about this time every day. You shall go with me, and we will get your trunk."

Mr. Presby took off his dressing gown, and, retiring to his chamber in the rear of the library, prepared himself for the ride. Bertha put on her hat and jacket again, and soon both were ready. Before they left, Mr. Presby gathered up some account books and papers that were on his desk, and placed them in a small iron safe in one corner of the room, which he locked, and put the key in his pocket.

The carriage was at the door, and Mr. Presby led the way downstairs. John was in the entry; but he was very obsequious this time, and bowed low as he opened the doors for them.

"Keep your eyes wide open, miss, or the old man will knock your brains out when he has the fit," he whispered in Bertha's ear, as she passed him.

"What do you mean?" asked she.

"Oh, Mr. Presby is stark, staring mad!" he replied, earnestly. "He will take your life before you have been with him three days."

Bertha's old fears assailed her again for a moment; but she could not believe, if Mr. Presby was such a dangerous person, that his friends would permit him to ride about the city without any attendant. They could have sent him to an asylum, for his family seemed to have no tender regard for him which would restrain them from such a course.

The carriage was driven to the station, and Bertha procured her trunk. It was placed in the little room adjoining the library, and then they were driven downtown. Mr. Presby visited several insurance offices, and other places of business, where he was treated with respect and consideration by all whom he met. Bertha entered several of the offices with him, and heard him talk about matters that were beyond her comprehension; but, very clearly, no one seemed to be of John's opinion, that Mr. Presby was "stark, staring mad."

On their return, at three o'clock, dinner was served. The table was prepared by a colored girl, who waited upon them, and removed the things when the meal was ended.

"Sylvia, is Mr. Presby—Edward—at home?" said the invalid to the girl, as she left the room with the dishes.

"Yes, sir."

"Has he dined?"

"Yes, sir."

"Tell him I wish to see him at his earliest convenience."

"I will, sir."

Bertha noticed that Mr. Presby's lips quivered as he spoke to the servant; and, as soon as she had gone, he seated himself in his chair, and appeared to be much agitated. In half an hour, during which time the old gentleman was silent and thoughtful, Edward Presby entered the room. He was a man of thirty-five, elegantly dressed, in whom an experienced observer would have detected what is called "a man of the world"—a man who lives for its pleasures alone, ignoring its cares and responsibilities.

"How do you do today, father?" said Edward, as he entered the room, and cast a searching glance at Bertha.

"I am as well as usual," replied the old man, coldly.

"You sent for me, father?"

"I did. John must be discharged."

Mr. Presby spoke these words with firmness, but his lip quivered, and his frame was slightly convulsed. It had evidently cost him a great effort to utter them.

"John—discharged?" repeated Edward Presby.

"He must be discharged," added the father.

"My wife would never consent to it. What has he done now?"

Mr. Presby explained the events of the morning; that John had refused to admit those who answered his advertisement; that he had told Bertha the "old man" was crazy.

"A mere pleasantry, father," replied Edward. "Probably John didn't know anything about the advertisement."

"Perhaps not. Does he believe that I am insane?"

"Of course not," laughed the son.

"Will you discharge him?"

"I couldn't think of such a thing. John is the most useful person in the house."

"Edward, I am in earnest. John must go, or I shall."

"Come, father, you are out of humor. Have you lost any money today?"

"I have nothing more to say, Edward," replied Mr. Presby, trembling with emotion.

"I am sure I haven't," added the son, as he withdrew.

The invalid went to his desk and wrote a few lines, which he inclosed in an envelope. Having written the direction upon it, he handed it to Bertha, and requested her to go down to Wall Street, and deliver it to the person for whom it was intended.

"I would not ask you to do such work for me if I could trust anyone else," said he, sadly.

"I will deliver the note," replied she.

"In a few days we will change our residence, Bertha," he added with a smile. "I hope in our new home we may be happier than we can be here."

Bertha knew not what to say, and therefore she said nothing. The father and the son did not agree, and the house was divided against itself. It was a very painful state of things to see this difference between those who should cherish and sustain each other, and Bertha, who had almost idolized her father, could not understand it. She put on her hat and jacket, and was leaving the room, when Mr. Presby called her back.

"If you stay with me, Bertha, you must understand all these things," said he. "It is a sad story to tell a young girl like you, but you must know it all. They will turn you against me, if you don't."

"No one shall turn me against you, sir. You have been very kind to me, and I am grateful for it."

"They will make you believe that I am crazy."

"I will not believe it, sir."

Mr. Presby seated himself again, and began to tell Bertha his troubles. He had two children, a son and a daughter. His wife had died ten years before, and soon after a difficulty between the father and son had occurred.

Edward had never devoted himself to business of any kind, but spent all his time in fashionable dissipation. He had married a gay and extravagant lady, and, after the death of his mother, he had been invited to "keep house" for his father. But the house was not large enough for the fashionable lady, and both she and Edward had importuned him to move into a magnificent palace of a house. Mr. Presby was simple in his tastes, and refused to do so. His refusal to comply had caused the first quarrel.

The daughter had joined with the son in the request to purchase the palace, and had taken sides with him in the quarrel. She desired to live in the style of a princess—to outdo all her neighbors and friends. The demands upon the purse of Mr. Presby became so extravagant that his fortune could not sustain such a pressure, and he had been compelled to limit the son to six thousand dollars a year, and the daughter to fifteen hundred.

Mr. Presby had been firm in his purpose, and every month he had paid over to each the sum allotted. He positively refused to grant another dollar, though he was continually annoyed by applications for more, which were often accompanied by threats and abusive language.

The quarrel had never been healed; on the contrary, the estrangement became greater every year. The son and his wife had obtained complete possession of the house, except the floor which the old gentleman had reserved for his own use. They managed its affairs to suit themselves, without even consulting his wishes or his tastes, and he soon felt himself a stranger there. They seemed to look forward with pleasure to the hour which would end his mortal pilgrimage, and place them in possession of his wealth.

Mr. Presby wept as he told this sad story, and Bertha pitied him more than ever. She thought he had been very liberal with his children, especially as the son refused to do any business, as his father wished. She could not see that he had been to blame, and she wondered at his patience.

"Now, Bertha, you understand it all," said he; "and I see that you pity me."

"I do, indeed."

"But they are my children, and I love them still. Oh, how it would gladden my heart to hear them speak gentle words to me! They hate me; they want my property, and would rejoice to have me die," groaned he, covering his face with his hands. "I would give all I have if they would love me."

"Perhaps they will."

"Their hearts are hardened against me. They want my money. And I would give it to them if it would make them love me. I would become a beggar for their sake. But they would spend all I have in a few years, and it would be folly to indulge them."

"I think John is a very bad man," said Bertha, recalling what he had said to her in the hall.

"He is not only a spy upon my actions, but he is employed to thwart me in my wishes. I cannot endure him. I have been peaceable and patient; but I cannot be so any longer. Now you may go with the note, Bertha."

"Shall I leave it if the gentleman is not in?"

"Yes; he will get it if it is left at his office."

"I will do so, sir."

"Stop a moment, Bertha. Have you any money to pay your fare?"

"Yes, sir; a little."

"Here is five dollars; you may wish to purchase something. You need not hurry back, for I shall try to sleep an hour or two, if I am not too much excited."

Bertha took the money, and thanked her employer for his kindness. As she descended the stairs, John was in his accustomed place; for no one seemed to pass in or out of the house without his knowledge.

"Where are you going, miss?" asked he, in conciliatory tones.

"I am going out," she replied, without stopping.

"So I see; but where are you going?"

"Downtown."

"Where?"

"Excuse me, John, but I am in a hurry to do my errand."

"What is your errand, miss?" persisted he.

"I do not think it proper to tell my employer's business to anyone, and you will excuse me if I do not answer you."

"Oh, certainly; it's none of my business, of course, and I did not mean to pry into the affairs of Mr. Presby."

Bertha placed her hand upon the door; but the night lock was a peculiar one, and she didn't understand it. She kept working upon it, and John did not offer to assist her.

"Have you seen Miss Ellen Presby?" asked John.

"I have not," replied Bertha, still trying to open the door.

"She wishes to see you. I will call her, if you please."

"I will see her when I return," said Bertha; but John had gone.

Bertha had some ingenuity, and before the man came back, she succeeded in opening the door. As she did so, she discovered a couple of night keys hanging near the door, and in order to save John the trouble of answering her summons, she put one of them in her pocket.

When she had seated herself in the car, she took out the note Mr. Presby had given her. She doubted not it had some reference to the matters which had transpired during the afternoon. She turned the envelope, and read with astonishment the name of the man, who, a few days before, had turned her out of Woodville. It was directed to "Samuel Grayle, Esq."

CHAPTER 17

SORELY PERSECUTED

Bertha was alarmed to find the name of Mr. Grayle on the note. She hoped Mr. Presby had no business relations with such a man, and she was frightened at the thought of seeing him again. He had insulted her at Woodville, and he might do so in New York. But her errand must be done; and she hoped he would not be in his office.

Mr. Grayle was in his private room with several gentlemen when she reached her destination. She gave the note to his clerk, and saw it delivered. It was a lucky escape, and she retreated from the place well satisfied with the result. As Mr. Presby had told her she need not hurry back, she decided to call upon Mr. Sherwood again.

"I'm very glad to see you again, Miss Grant," said the clerk, as she entered the office; "I have good news for you."

"Has my father got out of the Tombs?" asked Bertha, to whom this seemed to be the only good news that could come to her.

"No; not quite so good as that," replied the clerk, shaking his head. "You saw the gentleman who was with me when you left the office this morning?"

"I did."

"Did you know him?"

"I did not, though his face seemed strangely familiar."

"It was your uncle, from Valparaiso."

"Uncle Obed?"

"Yes, I suppose that is his name; at any rate, he is your father's only brother."

"Oh, I am so glad!" exclaimed Bertha, "for I know that he can save my father."

"Your father shall be saved, any way; but for the present your uncle cannot do much. He is a stranger in New York. His business in Valparaiso was entirely with English merchants."

"Where is he now?"

"He is stopping at the Astor House. If your father can be set at liberty, your uncle will take care of his pecuniary matters as soon as his funds arrive from England."

"I will call and see him."

"I think he has gone to Philadelphia, to see a friend who will furnish him with money to pay off your father's most pressing debts."

"That is just like Uncle Obed," said Bertha.

"He remained with me all the forenoon. He knows about Brace Brothers, and he says they have only suspended and will, eventually pay all they owe. If this is the case, Mr. Grant will yet come out all right. As the matter stands now, if your father could raise about fifty thousand dollars, it would keep him out of trouble till the affairs of Brace Brothers are settled up. This your uncle will endeavor to procure."

"Will Mr. Grayle be paid then?" asked Bertha.

"Mr. Grayle has already been paid. He has taken Woodville, though he says the estate will not pay him what he has advanced. I suppose it would not, if sold at auction, and he does not like the bargain. As soon as he pressed your father, and threw him into prison, others became clamorous for their money. I hope your uncle will be able to raise the sum needed."

"I am sure he will."

"He is very doubtful, for all his friends are in England, and all his property is there. He has retired from business, and means to settle in this vicinity, as soon as he can close up his affairs, and invest his wealth in this country. He was very anxious to see you."

"I will see him at once, if I can."

On her way uptown, she called at the Astor House; but Uncle Obed had gone to Philadelphia, as the clerk thought.

It was time for her to return to Mr. Presby's. Her father and his affairs now engrossed all her attention, and she even forgot those of her invalid employer. It was certainly good news that Uncle Obed had arrived. Her father had written to him several months before, and she had felt that, if he would come, all would be well. He could get Mr. Grant out of prison; he could recover possession of Woodville; and he could advance money to pay her father's debts, and thus save him from his creditors till the affairs of Brace Brothers were settled.

But Uncle Obed seemed to be almost powerless, after all. He had come, but he was a stranger in the land, with no means and no credit. He had wealth enough, but it might as well have been at the bottom of the Red Sea, so far as any present use was concerned.

Her father was still in prison.

Woodville was still in possession of Mr. Grayle.

Creditors representing fifty thousand dollars were still ready to harass her father.

Here were three tremendous obstacles in the path of her father. Bertha felt that she was but a child, and she could do nothing against such fearful odds; but still her mission was to save her father. The coming of Uncle Obed would keep the family from want; but all her father had seemed to be lost, and nothing but beggary or dependence to be before him. It was doubtful whether Uncle Obed could do anything before it was too late to save her father from ruin. What could she do herself? Alas! nothing.

Still thinking of these things, she arrived at the door of Mr. Presby's house. As she went up the stone steps, the thought came, that perhaps she might do something; but it was too absurd to be cherished, and she dismissed it at once. She was so absorbed with these reflections that she did not think of the night key in her pocket, and rang the bell. The summons was promptly answered by John, who opened the door about a foot, and placed himself in the aperture.

"Who do you wish to see, miss?" asked he, politely.

"I wish to see Mr. Presby—the old gentleman."

"Do you? Well, he isn't at home."

"Not at home?"

"He has just gone out of town, and won't be back for three days."

"If you will let me in, I will go to my room," said Bertha, who did not believe John's ridiculous story.

"Eh?" added the man, with a kind of leer, as though he did not understand her.

"I say I will go to my room, if you please."

"Your room? Pray, miss, where is your room?"

"It is the small chamber over the hall."

"Really, miss, I don't understand you. I don't see how your room can be in this house."

"Don't you know me, John?" asked Bertha, astonished at this singular reception.

"Don't I know you? How should I know you?" replied he, with an innocent look.

"I am the young lady Mr. Presby engaged today."

"Mr. Presby didn't engage any young lady today."

"Why, yes he did, John. You know me very well. Didn't you talk with me when I went out, two hours ago, and ask me where I was going?"

"I? 'Pon my word, I never saw you before in my life!" protested John, apparently amazed at this statement.

It was greeted by a loud laugh from the entry behind him. It was the same voice she had heard before, and Bertha supposed it must be Miss Ellen.

"Then, if you will call Mr. Presby, he will assure you I am the person he engaged."

"How can I tell him when he is out of town?"

"He is not out of town, John."

"Oh, now, that does not sound like a lady, to doubt my word; but I will call Mr. Edward Presby."

"I do not wish to see him."

"Then I can't do anything for you, miss."

"I will go up to my room."

"We don't let strangers into the house," replied John, decidedly.

"What do you mean, John? You know me well enough."

"Never saw you before in my life; and if you doubt my word, I shall never want to see you again."

"Send her away, John," said the female in the hall.

"Good evening, miss; if you call next week, you may see Mr. Presby," said John, with one of those wicked leers with which he accompanied his polite impudence, and closed the door in her face.

Bertha, astounded by this incident, retired from the door, and moved down the street again. Such villainy and such trickery were beyond her comprehension. She had actually been denied admission to the house of her employer. But she had spirit enough not to yield the point. She had walked down the street but a short distance before she thought of the night key in her pocket, and then she determined to return, and to make her way to Mr. Presby's library, whether John was willing or not, for it did not occur to her that he would carry his opposition so far as to prevent her by force from doing so. It was evident that Mr. Presby's son and daughter intended to prevent her from remaining with him. They feared her influence—that she might comfort and encourage the invalid, and thus prolong his life; or be an available witness in a contested will case; or that she might in some manner prevent them from controlling the old man's thoughts or actions. "You must not love me, or they will hate you," had been the warning of the father. If they wished to prevent her from seeing Mr. Presby again, it would be hard for her to do so.

Bertha felt that the old man was in the hands of his enemies, though they were his own children, and higher considerations than her own comfort and welfare prompted her not to yield to the conspiracy. She could not desert the old gentleman when he had been so kind to her. Obeying this generous impulse, she hastened up the steps, and inserted the night key as quickly as she could. The door was opened without difficulty, and, not stopping to close it, she hung up the night key on the nail from which she had taken it, and opened the inner door, intending to run upstairs before John should appear to dispute her passage.

She was partially successful, and had ascended a few steps before the vigilant manservant showed himself. But John, whom Mrs. Presby regarded as a useful person in the house, was as active as he was keen. No sooner did he discover that he had, in some mysterious manner, been circumvented, than he sprang up the stairs, and, catching hold of her dress, pulled her down to the door again.

"Who is it, John?" called the voice of the female from an adjoining room.

"It is the girl that tried to get in a few moments ago."

"A thief—isn't she, John?" said Mr. Edward Presby, who now appeared in the hall, followed by his wife and his sister.

"I suppose so, sir," replied the ready John. "She has been prowling about the house all day. I have sent her away twice."

"But how did she get in?" demanded Mr. Presby.

"That's more than I know; but this kind of folks always find a way to open a door," answered John, with a wicked grin.

"How did you get in?" said Mr. Presby, sternly.

"Hush, Ned," whispered Miss Ellen, pointing upstairs.

"No fear of him; he is fast asleep in the back chamber," muttered John.

But Mr. Presby acted upon this caution, and, taking Bertha by the arm, led her into the dining-room, in the rear, where the invalid could not hear what transpired.

"Now, how did you get in?" repeated Mr. Presby, in the same stern tone he had used before, as though he were speaking to a common thief, whom he hated and despised.

"I came in with the night key," replied Bertha, appalled at the turn which the affair had taken.

"Where did you get the night key?"

"I took it from the nail when I went out."

"When you went out! When was that?"

"I know what she means. She stole the key when she came to the door with the foolish inquiries," observed Miss Ellen.

"Did you miss the keys, John?" asked Mr. Presby.

"I did not, sir. I don't believe she got in that way. I will go and see;" and he left the room.

In a moment he returned, declaring the two night keys were hanging on the nail, where he had seen them half a dozen times during the day.

"She picked the lock, then," added Mr. Presby.

"Well, I hope something will be done about it this time," said Mrs. Presby. "You caught a woman in the hall once before, and let her go because she was well dressed."

"That was a mistake of mine; and I will not make another of the same kind. John, you may go for an officer."

"For mercy's sake, Mr. Presby, don't send me to prison!" said Bertha, terrified beyond expression.

"That is just what the woman said, in almost the same words," added Mrs. Presby.

"Don't you know me, sir?" pleaded Bertha. "I was in the library when you were there this afternoon."

"No use," replied Mr. Presby, shaking his head. "That kind of stuff won't go down."

"The other thief said she wanted to see her sister, who was a servant in the house," said Miss Ellen.

"It is a plain case, miss, and there is no use of wasting words in idle stories. I let one thief escape, and I will not permit another to slip through my fingers."

"I am no thief, sir. I beg you to send up to your father, and he will assure you I am not a thief," pleaded Bertha.

"My father is out of town."

Poor Bertha could say nothing to move her persecutors; and, in despair, she relapsed into silence. In a few moments John returned with a policeman. Mr. Presby and his man told their story, and the officer thought it was a very plain case.

"Come, miss," said he, taking her by the arm and leading her out into the street.

CHAPTER 18

BERTHA PROVES HER INNOCENCE

It was now quite dark, and in the friendly shades of night poor Bertha was spared the shame of being gazed upon by unthinking people in the street. The policeman took her by the hand, and conducted her to the station, where she was to remain till morning, when she would be taken before a magistrate to be examined on the charge of "breaking and entering."

She was so terrified by the scene through which she had just passed, that she had not the courage to say anything to the officers in vindication of her innocence. They looked at her with curiosity, and some of them seemed to regard her as a different person from those who were usually brought to the station.

"Bless my soul!" exclaimed a sergeant, when he came to look at her. "I have certainly seen that face before."

"Oh, Nathan!" groaned Bertha, as she recognized in the officer a man who had formerly been employed as coachman at Woodville.

"Bertha Grant!" ejaculated he, holding up both hands with astonishment. "It can't be possible!"

"I am innocent, Nathan," sobbed Bertha. "I have not done anything to bring me to this place."

"Poor girl! I can't do anything for you, I'm afraid."

"You will not keep me in this terrible place? You will not let them carry me before the court? It would kill my poor father."

"I would not, if I could help it, Bertha," replied Nathan, sadly; "but we have to keep people who are arrested on such charges till they are proved to be innocent."

"I am innocent! I have not done anything wrong."

"But I have no right to let you go—at least, while you stand charged with breaking and entering. If I dared, I would let you go at once."

"Let me tell you all about it, and then perhaps you will know what is best to be done."

"I will do everything I can for you, Bertha. You were always kind to me, and I would do anything to get you out of trouble."

"I don't want you to do wrong, Nathan. I would not have you neglect your duty even to save me from prison."

Bertha then told the sergeant everything that had occurred at the house of Mr. Presby during the day, from the moment she rang the bell in the forenoon till she had been taken out of the house by the policeman.

"Poor girl!" sighed the policeman, when she had finished her simple narrative. "I think we can get you out of trouble very soon. If Mr. Presby, the old gentleman, will only say that you were lawfully in the house, that you had a right to be there, we will not keep you a moment."

"Mr. Presby would come to me at once, if he only knew I was here; I know he would," added Bertha.

"It is a plain case, and all we want is a word from him. Now I will go right down to his house, and tell him all about it."

"I am afraid they will not let you see him."

"I will see him. Don't disturb yourself about that, Bertha. I shall certainly see him."

The sergeant then spoke to the principal officers of the station, and Bertha, instead of being put into a cell with the wretched thieves and drunkards who had already been brought in, was permitted to remain in the office.

At nine o'clock, Nathan had not returned, and Bertha was sure that he had found some difficulty in seeing Mr. Presby; but she was sure, too, that he would do all he could for her, and so she waited in hope and patience. Occasionally a thief or a vagabond was brought in, but Bertha did not even care to look at him. At ten o'clock, while she was wondering that the sergeant did not come, an officer led a boy into the room.

"What have you got there?" demanded the captain.

"A little fellow that I picked up in the next street. He is so tipsy he can't stand alone, and had stretched himself on the curbstone, where he was near having his legs broken by a carriage."

"Who is he?"

"Don't know, sir. He is well dressed. I asked him where his home was, and he said he hadn't any."

"No, sir," said the boy, rousing from his stupor, "I haven't any home; but I belong to the yacht *Whirlwind*."

"Merciful heavens!" cried Bertha, rushing to the side of the intoxicated youth.

"Do you know him, miss?" asked the captain.

"Yes, sir, I do," stammered Bertha.

"Who is he?"

"He is my brother."

"What! Is that you, Berty?" stammered Richard Grant. "Well, I am glad to see you, Berty. What are you doing here?"

"Oh, Richard!" was all that the poor girl could utter, as she threw herself into a chair, and wept bitterly.

"Put him to bed," said the captain, in a low tone.

The officers took the drunken boy out of his chair, and laid him in one of the bunks of an adjoining cell. The captain gave Bertha permission to stay with him, but he was unable to talk much, and soon dropped asleep. She covered him up, and seated herself by his side. When she heard the outer door open again, she hastened out to see if Nathan had come.

"Where is she? Poor child!" said Mr. Presby, as he entered the room.

Bertha hastened to him, her eyes still filled with the tears called forth by the new grief that had come upon her.

"Oh, I am so glad to see you, Mr. Presby!" exclaimed she, as she grasped the old gentleman's extended hands.

"Poor child! Poor child! I told you they would hate you if you loved me. They sent you to a prison—did they? Oh, God! They are my children."

"It's all right, Miss Bertha," said Nathan, who had already told the captain that the girl had spoken the truth.

"May Heaven bless you, Nathan!" said Bertha, taking him by the hand. "You have saved me from a world of anguish, and I shall be grateful to you as long as I live."

"Never mind that, Bertha. You were always good to me, and I am too glad of a chance to serve you."

"Poor child!" added Mr. Presby. "Are you satisfied now, captain?"

"Entirely; the girl can go as soon as she pleases," replied the captain.

"Come, Bertha, let us get away from this place; but we will remember your friend the sergeant. I have a carriage at the door. I will not let you go out of my sight again while we remain in the city. Come, Bertha."

"I can't go now," she replied, glancing at the cell in which Richard was sleeping off the fumes of the liquor he had drunk.

The captain now kindly came forward, and explained what had taken place during the absence of the sergeant. Mr. Presby was full of sympathy for the poor girl, and at once proposed to take Richard away with them; but Nathan promised to take care of him till morning, and detain him till Bertha could see him again.

"Now, Bertha, we will be happy," said Mr. Presby, when they were seated in the carriage. "I have just purchased a fine house in the country, and we will go there tomorrow. You shall not be persecuted any more."

"I do not care for myself," added Bertha.

"Your brother shall go with you. The poor boy had no home, and I suppose he was lonely. We will take care of him, and he will never do such a thing again."

"I hope not."

"The house I have bought is a beautiful one. I have purchased all the furniture, horses, boats, and everything, just as its late owner left it. I am sure we shall be very happy there."

"I hope you will be happy."

"I shall be; perhaps if I leave them, it will do them good. They do not believe that I will go, for I have threatened to do so a great many times. But the place is bought this time, and I have given my check for it. Did you think I never would come to you?"

"I thought John would not let the officer see you."

"I was not at home when he came. I was at Mr. Grayle's office, where the sale was completed, and the deed given."

"Mr. Grayle!" exclaimed Bertha, a new light appearing to her.

"Yes, Mr. Grayle; I bought the place of him. The estate is known by the name of Woodville. Quite a pretty name—isn't it?"

"Woodville!" repeated Bertha. "And you have bought it?"

"Yes; you appear to know the place."

"It was my home till a few days ago," answered Bertha, sadly.

"Your home! Good Heaven! Then you are the daughter of poor Franklin Grant."

"I am, sir."

"Poor child! I was slightly acquainted with your father; but he had a quarrel with Mr. Grayle, which concerned me, and I haven't seen him for several years."

"Is Mr. Grayle your friend?" asked she.

"Not exactly my friend. I have had some business relations with him; but I have nothing against your father."

Bertha, in her own simple style, then told him what Mr. Grayle had done to her father, and that he had turned his children out of Woodville. Mr. Presby was indignant, and declared that he would never trust him again.

When the carriage reached the house, they were admitted by John, who was as polite as a French dancing master. They had no sooner entered the library than Edward Presby presented himself. He declared that the arrest of Bertha was a mistake. He did not know her, and none of the family had ever seen her.

"Edward," said the father, sternly, "it is useless for you to say anything. We part tomorrow; let it be in peace."

"Part, father?" exclaimed Edward.

Mr. Presby briefly informed his son what he had done, and stated his plans for the future.

"Surely you will not leave us, father," said Edward, who probably began to realize that he had gone too far.

"I shall go tomorrow."

The son tried to explain, and said all he could to alter his purpose; but Mr. Presby remained firm to the last, and he finally retired in anger, and with threats on his lips.

Bertha went to her chamber, but she could not sleep, she was so excited by the events of the evening. On the morrow she was to return to Woodville, though not with the family; and she was sad at the thought of going without her father.

Uncle Obed would return from Philadelphia the next day, and she hoped he would bring some comfort for her; for with Richard intoxicated in the station house, and her father still in the Tombs, her mission seemed further than ever from its accomplishment.

CHAPTER 19

UNCLE OBED

Mr. Presby called Bertha at an early hour on the following morning, for the carriage had been engaged for her at seven o'clock. She had slept but little during the night, for the terrible condition of her brother haunted her thoughts when awake, and her dreams when she slept. She was driven to the station house, where Richard had slept off the fumes of the intoxicating cup.

He was glad to see her, but he was very much depressed in spirits, and heartily ashamed of his conduct. He was more reasonable and penitent than she had ever seen him before. He told her that the yacht had come from Newport the day before, and that he had been discharged, because they no longer wanted him. He had taken a room at a hotel, but he had only two dollars left of the money he had brought from Woodville, increased by a few dollars he had earned. He acknowledged that he had been intoxicated twice while at Newport, and when he came to New York he felt sad at the thought of having no home; and he had drunk some wine to cheer him up, and make him forget that his father was in prison, and the family scattered.

"Bertha, I never will taste any wine or liquor again as long as I live," said he, with solemn earnestness, when he had finished his narrative.

"I hope you never will, Richard. My heart is nearly broken now," added Bertha, wiping away her tears; "but if you will be good and true, I shall be happy again. Oh, you don't know how much I have thought of you!"

"Come, Berty, don't cry. I have been selfish, but I will stand by you to the last. I will do anything you wish."

Bertha was very much comforted by Richard's promises of amendment, for she felt that he meant them, and she prayed that he might have the firmness to keep them. She then told him what had happened during their separation; of the sale of Woodville, and the return of Uncle Obed, and that she was going to their old home with Mr. Presby.

This conversation took place in the carriage, and on the sidewalk in front of Mr. Presby's house. For some time, Richard could not be persuaded to visit his sister's employer; but he at last consented. The old gentleman did not allude to the events of the preceding evening, but talked about his plans in connection with Woodville. He insisted that Richard should go with them, and occupy his old room; indeed, he said he wanted him very much to assist him in finding the housekeeper, the boatman, and the servants, for he intended to restore everything to the condition in which Mr. Grant had left it.

Richard gladly consented to remain and assist him in moving his books, papers, and other articles, which were to be conveyed to Woodville. His wonted spirits seemed to return when his mind was occupied, and before breakfast was over Mr. Presby and Richard were excellent friends.

The forenoon was occupied in packing up the books and papers, which were sent off early in the afternoon, under the care of Richard, who had instructions to find the old servants and send them back to their accustomed places.

At one o'clock, when the Philadelphia train had arrived, Bertha repaired to the Astor House, to ascertain if Uncle Obed had returned, leaving Mr. Presby with his son and daughter. The latter were astonished and alarmed at the firmness of their father, and the events of years were rehearsed and commented upon. They promised to let him have his own way in all things if he would remain, and were even willing to discharge John. They asked him what the world would say; but he was silent. They proposed to go with him to Woodville; but he declined. He had gone too far to recede. Mr. Presby told them what he had suffered, but he spoke kindly, and hoped they would visit him in his new home.

Bertha was rejoiced to find that Uncle Obed was in the house, and she was shown to his room. She had never seen him before they met in the office of her father, but the picture of him that hung in the drawing room at Woodville was so true that his countenance seemed familiar to her.

"My dear uncle!" exclaimed she, as she rushed forward to grasp his extended hand.

"Then this is Bertha," replied Uncle Obed, kissing her.

"I am so glad to see you!"

"And I am as glad to see you; for when I heard what had happened, I was very much alarmed about you."

Of course the conversation immediately turned to the situation of her father. Bertha told him what had occurred from the time of her father's arrest. Uncle Obed was sad and thoughtful. He was perplexed and disappointed. He felt a strong desire to do something which he could not accomplish.

"Mr. Sherwood told me you had gone to Philadelphia to obtain the money which would save my poor father from ruin," said Bertha.

"I did go, but my friend was not at home, and will not return for a week. Bertha, I am sorely tried; I don't see that I can do anything for your father at present. I cannot raise the money."

"I hoped you would be able to save my poor father."

"I have done everything I could; but I am a stranger here now. Fifty thousand dollars is an immense sum of money."

"Perhaps I can raise it, Uncle Obed," said Bertha, musing.

"You, child? Of course you cannot."

"I can try."

Uncle Obed laughed at the assurance of Bertha, and did not bestow a second thought upon the absurd proposition.

"I must go to Woodville with Mr. Presby this afternoon," said she, "and I must leave you now, uncle."

"I am sorry Woodville was sold, for I meant to buy it myself when my funds arrive. I intended to have seen Mr. Grayle yesterday. I suppose it is of no use to regret it, though. When shall I see you again, Bertha?"

"I shall probably come to the city tomorrow with Mr. Presby."

Bertha hastened back to the house of Mr. Presby, where he was to wait her return.

"Did you see your uncle?" asked he.

"Yes, sir."

"You told me he would release your father."

"Yes, sir; but he cannot," replied Bertha, bursting into tears.

"Poor child! Why not?"

"Mr. Grayle put my father in prison, and keeps him there."

"I will see Grayle before I go to Woodville," said the old gentleman, jumping out of his chair.

"But that would not be enough," added Bertha.

"What more, child?"

"My uncle has been trying to raise a large sum of money to satisfy the creditors who persecute my father."

"How much money?"

"Fifty thousand dollars," replied Bertha, drawing a very long breath.

"Fifty thousand!" exclaimed Mr. Presby.

"My uncle will be responsible for it; he is a rich man, but all his wealth is in England."

"You shall have the money, my child," said Mr. Presby, after a few moments' consideration.

"May Heaven bless you as you have blessed me!" exclaimed Bertha, clasping his hands and kissing his forehead.

"I will go down now and see Grayle; then I will meet you at the Astor House. It will be late when we get to Woodville tonight, but your father shall go with us, Bertha," said the old gentleman, as he put on his hat and took his cane. "Come, child; we will lose no time."

"Oh, sir, I am so happy!"

"I didn't understand before that Grayle caused your father to be imprisoned. If I had, I would have seen him before."

Bertha hastened back to the Astor House, while Mr. Presby took a carriage and drove to the office of Grayle.

"Oh, Uncle Obed!" cried Bertha, as she rushed into his room, out of breath with the exertion of running upstairs.

"What now, Bertha?"

"I have got the money!"

"What! Impossible!"

"I have; Mr. Presby will let you have it, and father will be set at liberty tonight!"

Uncle Obed was incredulous, and seemed to be of John's opinion, that Mr. Presby was crazy. He absolutely refused to believe the good news, and the nonappearance of Mr. Presby seemed to justify his want of faith. It was three hours before the old gentleman came, and Bertha began to fear that her enthusiasm had deceived her. But he came at last, and the two gentlemen were introduced to each other.

Mr. Presby opened the business of the meeting by saying what a good girl Bertha was; that, though he had known her only two days, he loved her as his own child. He then inquired particularly into Uncle Obed's business affairs, and having satisfied himself in regard to his financial soundness, he produced checks for fifty thousand dollars.

"Business men would call me a fool or a lunatic, after what I have done; but if I knew I should lose every dollar I have advanced, I should do just as I have done," said Mr. Presby, placing Uncle Obed's notes in his pocket-book.

"You shall not lose a penny of it, Mr. Presby," said Uncle Obed. "I can pay these notes three times over."

"I don't doubt it, Mr. Grant. Now, if the business is finished, we will call in somebody else," added Mr. Presby, as he rang the bell.

He whispered something very mysteriously to the bell boy who answered the summons and then continued the conversation with Uncle Obed.

"I have purchased your brother's estate—Woodville; but whenever he wants it again, he shall have it," said he. "I must be in sight of Bertha; and I suppose I can buy a piece of land and build a cottage upon it."

"Nay, sir, you shall always have a home at Woodville. I can promise that for my brother," replied Uncle Obed.

"Oh, yes!" said Bertha. "I should be so happy to have you at our house!"

"Brace Brothers will certainly pay all they owe. I fully understand the cause of their suspension. When your father gets out of this difficulty, he will be as well off as ever he was," added Uncle Obed.

At this moment the door was thrown open by the waiter. A joyful cry from Bertha revealed the nature of Mr. Presby's mysterious proceedings with the bell boy.

"My father! My father!" exclaimed Bertha, as she rushed into his arms, and kissed him over and over again.

"My dear child!" said Mr. Grant, as he pressed the overjoyed daughter to his heart, while the great tears rolled down his thin, pale cheek.

Bertha felt that her mission was accomplished—at least her present and most urgent one. Tenderly caressing her father, she told him how kind Mr. Presby had been to her.

"This is all Bertha's work, Franklin," said Uncle Obed. "She raised the money, and procured your release."

"No, father; it was Mr. Presby."

"For your sake I did it, my child," added Mr. Presby. "But come; we are all going to Woodville tonight."

The next train bore the whole party from the city. On the way all the incidents connected with the release of Mr. Grant were rehearsed. At first Grayle would not consent to it; but Mr. Presby had compelled him to do so by threats which he had the power to carry out, for the wretch owed him large sums of money. Mr. Presby had become his bail till the action could be disposed of; but Grayle admitted that the charge of fraud couldn't be proved. He declared that the affair would ruin him when Mr. Grant was released.

It was dark when the party arrived at Woodville; but the house was lighted up, and they were greeted by the housekeeper and the old boatman, whom Richard had summoned back to the mansion. Noddy Newman turned half a dozen back somersets on the lawn when he saw Bertha running up the walk. Several of the servants were in their places, and dinner was on the table, just as though no break had occurred in the household arrangements. Ben was sent after Fanny, and that evening the family were reunited in the sitting-room.

CHAPTER 20

BERTHA VISITS THE GLEN AGAIN

The next day Mr. Grant and Uncle Obed went to the city to arrange the business of the former, leaving Mr. Presby at home with the children. Bertha spent the whole forenoon in showing the old gentleman about the estate, and leading him to all the pleasant places in the vicinity.

After luncheon, Richard took them over to Whitestone in the *Greyhound*, and on their return they visited Van Alstine's Island and the Glen. Even Dunk's Hollow had heard the glad tidings of the return of the family to Woodville, and the children of the little mission school had gone to the Glen in the forenoon, and again in the afternoon, in the hope that Bertha might meet them there.

As the party landed, they were received with shouts of rejoicing. Gretchy von Brunt danced with joy, and Grouty von Grunt leaped up in the air as though the ground had been too hot to stand upon, while the other members of the school manifested their satisfaction in a manner not less equivocal, though rather more dignified. Bertha kissed all the children, boys and girls; for they all had clean faces, and wore the new clothes which their teacher had provided.

The whole troop ran before Bertha as she conducted Mr. Presby up to the Glen, and seated themselves in their accustomed places in the arbor. The visitors spent a very pleasant hour with them, and left, with the promise to come again on the following day.

"Now, Bertha, you must go on with your school, just as you did before," said Mr. Presby. "If the children want clothes or books, or anything costing money, you must let me know. And you must let me help you teach the school."

"Thank you, sir. It is very kind of you to feel an interest in these poor children," replied Bertha.

"It will make me happy, as it does you. Of course your school can last only four or five months?"

"No, sir; it is too cold after October to meet at the Glen."

"Well, Bertha, we must build a nice little schoolhouse, so that we can meet the children in the winter."

As the boat bore them down to the Woodville landing, Mr. Presby and Bertha formed many plans for improving the condition of the poor children of Dunk's Hollow; but the limit of our story does not permit us to follow them in the execution of those notable schemes. The little schoolhouse was built; other children were induced to join the number; all the scholars were supplied with warm clothing for the winter; and as the pupils could all read very well, a library was provided for their use. From the children, the mission of Bertha and her wealthy colaborer extended to the parents, and Dunk's Hollow itself began to wear a new aspect. Mr. Presby talked with the men, and many of them changed their modes of life and became decent, not to say respectable, persons.

Such was the result of Bertha's mission to the poor children of Dunk's Hollow.

Mr. Grant made satisfactory arrangements with his creditors. Brace Brothers, as Uncle Obed and others had anticipated, paid their debts in full; and the money which Mr. Presby had advanced was not only refunded, but Woodville was bought back again, and Mr. Grant was congratulated by all his friends and neighbors upon the happy termination of his troubles.

The only person who seemed to be a permanent sufferer by the transactions we have described was Mr. Grayle. His conduct in causing the arrest of the broker was generally condemned, for he was actuated by revenge and a desire to make money out of the misfortunes of others. As Mr. Sherwood had predicted, his course proved to be his ruin; for when the whole truth came out at a meeting of Mr. Grant's creditors, a storm of indignation was raised against him. Losing the respect and confidence of business men, he failed, and sought a new home in the West to retrieve his fallen fortunes.

When Woodville again came into the possession of Mr. Grant, and his credit was completely restored, a great dinner party was given in honor of the event. Among those invited were Mr. and Mrs. Byron, as well as Mr. Gray, and others who had attended on the memorable occasion when Master Charley had made a sensation. Strange as it may seem, Mrs. Byron came; and when she saw the gentle girl, whom she had insulted and turned out of her house, honored and respected by the most distinguished people in the vicinity, she blushed with shame.

Master Charley Byron, who always had his own way, insisted upon paying a visit to his former governess on this occasion; and, of course, he came. Bertha sang "Three Blind Mice" to him, and Noddy Newman turned a hundred back somersets on the lawn for his special benefit; but Charley was too wise to attempt the feat himself. The heir of Blue Hill could spell "cat" and "dog," but he had made no further progress in knowledge; and it is not at all probable that he will ever be President of the United States.

At other times, there came to Woodville Mrs. Lamb, Peter, the head groom of Blue Hill, and his wife; Nathan, the sergeant of police; Bob Bleeker, and others who had befriended Bertha in her want and peril. They were kindly received, and encouraged to continue in the faith that those who assist the needy shall not lose their reward.

Mr. Sherwood was a frequent visitor at Woodville, and his fidelity to his employer was so highly appreciated, that he soon became the partner of the broker; and a few years later, when Mr. Grant retired, he succeeded to the entire business.

Noddy Newman was as full of "antics" as he had ever been; and when Ben, the boatman, returned to his old position at Woodville, the little savage came with him. But he was under the influence of Bertha, who still persevered in her efforts to make a civilized man of him.

Mr. Presby proposed to build a cottage for himself near the mansion house, but neither Bertha nor her father would permit him to leave the family. An addition was made to the house, which afforded him a suit of rooms, and every day Bertha wrote his letters and read to him. The old gentleman increased the allowances of his son and daughter. They occasionally made him a visit at his new home, and though they still hungered for his money, they could not now do otherwise than treat him with respect, and even with a show of affection.

Removed from his troubles, and surrounded by genial and loving friends, Mr. Presby ceased to be an invalid, and lived ten years after his removal to Woodville. When he died, Bertha Grant was made rich; several charitable institutions received large donations; but the ungrateful son and daughter did not obtain the rest; for it was left in charge of trustees, who were instructed to pay them only the income of it during their lives, the principal to be equally divided among their children when they reached their majority.

Richard Grant, I am sorry to say, we must leave as we began with him. Even the bitter experience at Newport and New York was not enough to reform his life and character. He is almost the only trial of Bertha and her father, though they hope and pray that he will yet become a good and true man.

Miss Fanny's pride, after its sudden fall, was more moderate and reasonable, though there was still much to hope for, and, better yet, much to expect from the improvement already made. We are happy to inform her sympathizing young friends, that, when her next birthday was celebrated, all who were invited attended her party.

Ben, the boatman, almost worships "Miss Bertha." As he grows older, and his rheumatism becomes more troublesome, he finds in her a constant friend, who chooses never to forget his devotion to her in the dark hour of trial and sorrow. He is still a strict disciplinarian, and, though he makes Noddy "stand round," he likes the boy, and feels a deep interest in his future welfare.

Bertha's mission is still unfinished; for as fast as one good work is accomplished, another presents itself. The willing heart and ready hand can never want a field of labor. "Whatsoever our hands find to do, let us do it with all our might," and then we shall realize the happiness which crowned the mission of Bertha Grant.

www.ingramcontent.com/pod-product-compliance
Lightning Source LLC
Chambersburg PA
CBHW011437170626
46808CB00009B/3083

* 9 781667 641027 *